The Governor's Prisoner

The Governor's Prisoner

Roy E. Young

Old Mountain Press

Published by:
Old Mountain Press, Inc.
2542 S. Edgewater Dr.
Fayetteville, NC 28303

www.oldmp.com

© 1999 Roy E. Young

ISBN: 1-884778-72-0
Library of Congress Catalog Card Number: 99-63875

The Governor's Prisoner.

First Edition
Manufactured in the United States of America
1 2 3 4 5 6 7 8 9 10

In appreciation to God, and the great State of North Carolina, for allowing a weak child to grow strong.

To my brother John Calvin for always being there for me.

To William Appleby of Gouverneur, NY for his encouragement, support, and expertise in editing this novel.

To Joseph C. Pistolesi, and family, of Gouverneur, NY for many years of friendship and always making this southerner feel at home although I was a thousand miles from home.

Lastly, to the many who have read this novel and enjoyed it. Thank you for the many wonderful comments.

Chapter I

The Trial

"O judgment! Thou art fled to brutish beasts,
And men have lost their reason!" Shakespeare

The man's name was Wadus Strickland. He stood in the crowded Superior Courtroom in Smithfield, North Carolina. He faced an elderly judge whose wrinkled face and silver hair spoke of the many years and mental weight of the judgments he had rendered which had determined the lives of so many. Wadus Strickland stood silently, with head lowered, as the judge spoke.

"Mr. Strickland you are charged with two counts of assault with a deadly weapon with the intent to kill. How do you plead to these charges?"

There was nothing very impressive about the physical appearance of the man to whom the judge spoke. He stood six feet tall, 130 to 135 pounds, dark eyes, rapidly graying hair and appeared to be in his late forties. There was, however, an inner impressiveness the keen eye, and mind seemed to sense, yet could not verbalize. He had an interesting face. This face seemed to be sending silent, and sad, messages about the life of a common man. He was like millions of other common men who were taken for granted and forgotten a million times each day across the land. It was indeed a loud silence and one felt as if he were shouting for millions of others who wanted to say, "I am here but you do not see me, you do not hear me, you do not know me, to you I do not exist!"

7

Looking up Wadus Strickland replied to the judge's question, "I plead guilty sir."

Judge Harrison sat silently and stared down at Wadus Strickland and then began to turn the pages of the file before him.

"Mr. Strickland, do you fully understand the seriousness of the charges, and consequences, which you are facing?"

Wadus Strickland indicated he did understand by simply nodding his head and the judge quickly demanded, "Say yes, or no, for the court records."

Wadus answered with another nod and said, "Yes sir, I do understand."

Judge Harrison once again hesitated, looked downward and slowly ran his fingers through his long silver hair. Finally he raised his head, looked sternly at the prosecuting attorney, and commanded, "Counselor approach the bench please."

The Assistant District Attorney for Johnston County rose and walked quickly until he stood directly in front of the judge. Leaning forward Judge Harrison spoke in a low but strong tone, "Why is this man not represented by legal counsel?"

"Your honor he has, in the last several months, been offered representation several times but each time has refused to be represented. He maintains it is equally his right to choose not to have counsel as it is his right to have counsel. He has insisted upon pleading guilty as charged. Sir, I do not know why, but based upon my past interviews with this man he seems to want to go to jail."

"Have you fully, and clearly, explained that if he pleads guilty the court must hand down the maximum sentence?"

The attorney quickly answered, "Yes your honor I have, as well as a public defender and two other attorneys who have offered to represent him free of charge. Your honor, evidently this man has much support because a great deal of money has been raised for his defense. He has refused to access any of this money for that purpose and has rejected every other offer of help. He even refused to request bail!"

"Yes, I know he has been in custody for several months. I am further aware of the events, which led to these charges, and I am not comfortable with this case! Now, has he been psychologically examined to determine if he is mentally sound,

8

mentally capable enough to understand the consequences of the decision he is making?"

"Yes, indeed sir. He has been psychologically tested by three certified, and expert, psychologists."

"Well, what was their certified expert opinions?"

"Your honor, after extensive examinations of this man each doctor independently came to the same basic conclusion. They determined that he was not only sane, but also his mental aptitude falls within the top tenth percentile of the population. His ability to reason, his awareness, powers of observation, and level of self-actualization are quite rare. One doctor even stated this man would have no problem becoming a MENSA member if he desired to do so."

"Enlighten my tired and archaic mind. What is MENSA?"

"Sir, it is an international society of brilliant persons. Very few persons are able to mentally qualify."

"I see, return to your seat." The large courtroom was crowded but unusually quiet as the judge leaned back into his chair, folded his arms, and stared at the man upon whom he was forced to render judgment. Finally he asked, "Mr. Strickland, once again I am inclined to ask you if it is your intent, and desire, to plead guilty to these charges?"

Once again Wadus Strickland nodded and said, "Yes your honor, it is."

"Mr. Strickland, under the circumstances and for the benefit of my own conscience, I must know why you choose to do so? Why have you refused counsel? Why are you unwilling to speak-up in defense of yourself? Why have you refused to be judged by a jury of your peers? It is almost certain that a jury's verdict would be more lenient than the one I must render under the letter of the law."

At this point Wadus Strickland slowly raised his head and stared directly into the face of Judge Harrison for the first time. Without evident emotion, or regret, of what was to come, he replied, "Because I did what I am charged with. Because I am guilty!"

"Do you understand that under the circumstances, and considering your age, if you live you will likely be an old man by the time you are released from prison?"

"Yes sir, I do understand."

A long moment of silence followed as the judge lowered his head into his hands and raked his aged fingers through his long silver hair as if hoping for an escape, an answer, a reason why he would not be forced to render a judgment in this case.

"Mr. Strickland, I understand you are an educated man, is that correct?"

"I have the degrees sir."

"What did you do for a livelihood?"

"I was a school teacher."

"A teacher. How many years have you taught?"

"Twenty eight years."

"What subject and at what level did you teach?"

"I taught at the high school level. I taught political science, global studies, European history, sociology and psychology."

"Psychology—, Mr. Strickland what is MENSA?"

"It's supposed to be a group of smart people."

"Doesn't sound as though you have much faith in these MENSA people that are supposed to be so intelligent."

"Intelligence is a relative thing sir."

Judge Harrison again paused and slowly turned the pages of the file that was before him and told another story. What he read would not be heard, or considered, unless the man who stood before him changed his plea.

The Assistant District Attorney was growing increasingly annoyed by the delay and rose from his chair. "Your honor, a plea of guilty has been entered by the defendant, all proper legal procedures have been followed, and he has had repeated opportunities to change his plea and still does. At this point I see little point, or reason, to postpone and drag-out this case any longer. Especially considering the volume of cases pending before this court."

Judge Harrison quickly responded, "Counselor, considering I am your senior chronologically, professionally, and authoritatively, I strongly suggest that you not attempt to lecture me as to the progress, procedure, time, or case load which exist in this court! Do you understand me counselor?"

"Yes sir your honor I do. I apologize sir."

The Judge once again focused his attention upon the defendant and said, "Mr. Strickland, I have spent close to a half of a century in the legal profession. I have sat upon the bench as a judge for over two decades. I do not think I have ever faced a situation such as you have presented me with. You are forcing me to render a verdict, dictated by the strict letter of the law. It troubles me deeply, and such an old man does not need such troubles, but you give me no alternative! The North Carolina legal code gives me no alternative! You give me no choice and I feel trapped. Mr. Strickland, look at me!"

Wadus Strickland raised his head and gazed into the eyes of the man who would now determine his future. Judge Harrison spoke in a firm tone, "Wadus Strickland you have pleaded guilty to two counts of assault with a deadly weapon with the intent to kill. You are sentenced to serve thirteen years in the state prison for each of these charges. You will immediately begin serving the second sentence upon completion of the first. You are to be immediately transported to Central Prison in Raleigh where you will serve this sentence."

The Judge sat for what seemed to be a much longer time but was only moments and said, "This decision has given me no pleasure or satisfaction and I hope God may be with you in the coming years." With a loud rap of his gavel he pronounced, "Court closed."

The judge slowly rose from his chair as if burdened by some great weight. The bailiff shouted, "All rise." Everyone stood and silently watched the judge's slow exit through a door in the rear of the courtroom.

Chapter 2

The Visit
*"There is no death! The stars go down
to rise upon some other shore,
And bright in Heaven's jeweled crown,
They shine for ever more."* John L. McCreery

Two North Carolina State troopers approached each side of Wadus Strickland. One grasped his left arm and the other his right arm as they led him through the back of the courthouse where a patrol unit was waiting for this passenger.

The large trooper's name tag read "Captain Stewart" and he appeared to be in his early fifties. The younger trooper's tag simply read "M. Henderson" and he was obviously new to the field of law enforcement. Captain Stewart was a well-known, and highly respected, officer who had established his reputation in different areas of the state but had served in Johnston County for many years.

Captain Stewart opened the back door of the silver and black patrol unit and the rookie Henderson forcefully pressed the head of Wadus downward while aggressively shoving him into the back seat and slamming the door. Captain Stewart stared silently, and sternly, with obvious disapproval of his partner's unnecessary macho attitude. Stepping by the young trooper, the captain opened the door again and ordered, "lean forward." He then removed the handcuffs from behind the prisoner and handcuffed him again with his arms in front. He said, "That should feel a little better." He then instructed

Wadus to move to the right side so he could be seen in the rear view mirror. Henderson said, "Captain, I'll drive."

"No, I want to, I don't mind."

The captain exited the parking lot and drove slowly out of Smithfield onto highway 210. At this turn the rookie officer turned quickly and said, "Captain, you took the wrong turn, we should go out and pick up route 70. It's a much shorter way." Without turning Captain Stewart said, "Yes, I know, but we can go over to Interstate 40 and make better time."

Wadus sat silently in the back seat as if drugged and gazed out of the window to his right. After traveling almost three miles on Rt. 210, the automobile slowed and turned to the right onto a little traveled rural county road. Suddenly Wadus Strickland came-out of his zombie like state of mind, and turning his head quickly he met the eyes of Captain Stewart in the rear view mirror staring back at him as if to send a silent message. Wadus received his message! His heart raced, and although his eyes glistened with tears, he anticipated a moment of joy he had not expected and knew he might never again have. He felt an unspoken but sincere bond with the veteran officer.

As the patrol unit had begun to deviate from its intended route young Henderson immediately turned and said, "Captain, where are you going?" Receiving no reply he added, "Look Captain, I don't understand this and it is highly irregular."

"Relax Henderson, I'll have you back by the time your shift ends. Besides it's a beautiful day to see the autumn colors." Henderson was clearly not pleased and pouted silently.

It was mid-October and the trees were gently swaying as if dancing joyfully in their new brilliant fall costumes of many colors.

After traveling almost a mile and a half Captain Stewart pulled to the side of the road and killed the engine. There were no houses, barns, or animals to be sighted in any direction. Henderson surveyed all of the surroundings trying to determine where he was and what was taking place.

Wadus focused his attention to the slightly rising field that bordered a forest almost four hundred yards away. He turned quickly as Captain Stewart spoke as if speaking through the

13

mirror looked at Wadus and asked, "Strickland, do you want to do this?"

"Oh yes sir, very much!"

Exiting the patrol unit, Captain Stewart walked around and opened the back door as Henderson shook his head showing his concern and disapproval. The Captain helped Wadus exit the unit and said, "Strickland, we don't have much time so you're gonna have to get right on up there."

Henderson looked in all directions and wondered where "up there" was as he watched Wadus cross a small ditch embankment and enter the field. He could no longer restrain his frustration and began to protest. "Captain, just what in hell is going on? You're in violation of departmental procedure not to mention you're making it possible for this prisoner to escape!"

Captain Stewart did not turn toward Henderson as he watched Strickland walk a few yards into the field. He called to Wadus from behind, "Strickland, are you gonna run?"

Without turning the handcuffed man replied, "No sir", and continued his trek upward toward the tree line.

"Come on Henderson we'll follow close behind him if it will make you feel better. Besides, I'll bet a young man like you might even be able to outrun a man of his age. Considering he's wearing handcuffs, you might even be able to out wrestle him."

"Captain Stewart I resent that."

"Oh hell trooper, relax before you get the drizzles."

As Wadus Strickland increased his pace toward the colorful tree line an object at the edge of the field began to shine in the distance.

Henderson asked, "Well, where's he going?"

Captain Stewart pointed straight ahead up the hill where the shinning object could now be identified as a small marble gravestone. Wadus approached the white stone as if confronting God, his soul, and all of the universe combined. Captain Stewart put his arm out and stopped Henderson. They both stood silently about fifteen yards behind their prisoner.

Wadus Strickland's vision was blurred by tears as he read the inscription on the marble stone. It read, "James Edward Strickland, 1975-1988, Beloved Son of Mary and Wadus

Strickland, We shall find you." The strength rushed from his body and Wadus sank to his knees and lowered his head. In an instant, his mind, and view, was catapulted back to the afternoon of June the thirteenth. As he drove into the driveway of his ex-wife's home he saw his beautiful son waiting on the porch. He came running down the driveway dressed in his Little League baseball uniform and carrying his bat and glove. Wadus greeted his son with a firm hug and joyous smile. His son said, "Come on Dad, I'll be late for the game."

"O.K., O.K. son, we're on our way," and he backed his car out of the driveway. They had both laughed and talked rapidly en route to the game field. His Jamie was to be the starting pitcher that day. They were about one mile from their destination when he remembered seeing an object from the corner of his eye. He was still talking with his son as the object struck with comet speed and force! Wadus's head shattered the side window, his body slammed into the steering column and dashboard as the automobile made several complete circles and then crashed into a telephone pole on his son's side of the vehicle. He tried desperately to move but could not for several moments and in his semi-conscious state felt the blood from his forehead stream down across his face. Finally being able to move he began shouting, "Jamie, Jamie, Jamie," to his son who lay slumped over, motionless, as he leaned against the door quiet and still as if in a deep sleep. Gathering all of his strength he pulled his son to him and out of the driver's side of the car. Still shouting his son's name, he began a frantic but futile attempt to revive his beautiful little son. There was no response. As a crowd began to gather, Wadus could hear voices over to his right. They were laughing! Wiping the blood from his eyes he could see two young men standing in front of their badly damaged convertible sports car. They appeared to be very amused and one said, "Holy shit, look at this friggin mess!" His companion replied with laughter, "Who gives a rat's ass, your old man'll get you another one tomorrow." Wadus saw his son's aluminum bat on the car seat and grasped it by the small end. With all the strength he could summon he slowly rose to his feet and staggered toward the two young men who were still amusing themselves with their wrecked

15

sports car. As the one standing in front of the car turned his head to face Wadus he had a millisecond image of the bat before it violently smashed into his nose and upper teeth. While he went screaming to the ground in great pain Wadus struck the second young man across both shins breaking both of the bones. Both young men screamed in agony, but Wadus could only see his son's body lying very still only feet away. Twice more he raised the bat and struck one across the ribcage and then his kneecaps. Stepping deliberately, but slowly, to the next he shattered the man's shoulder. He was extremely dizzy, and unstable, as he stood straddling the one who had been driving the sports car. He raised the bat far above his head and started a downward swing, with all his strength, toward the man's head. His swing was abruptly halted by two large, and powerful arms, wrapping around him from the rear. They were the arms of Captain Stewart who was the first officer at the scene of the accident.

James Edward Strickland was dead on arrival at Johnston County Hospital. He had died instantly of a broken neck. Two days later he was buried here in this large field owned by his mother's father. This spot was chosen because he had loved it so much. He came here often with Wadus, and they had spent many happy days walking in the woods and resting in the edge of the field. A giant oak in the edge of the field had been spared because of its beauty and had watched on many occasions as father and son had talked, eaten, and napped under its majestic branches. It now stood watch over this small white stone and the little boy beneath.

Wadus Strickland was indicted and placed in the Johnston County jail. He was not allowed to attend his son's funeral, not that he could have for he had to be medicated and was so sedated that for days he was almost comatose and in a semiconscious state. It was a nightmare only he would ever know and one which would have totally destroyed the mind of most. For days he thrashed about as if tied, and weighted down, on the bottom of a deep pool. No matter how desperately he fought to come to the surface he could not! No matter how hard he had gasped for air he could not breathe! He could not rise. He could not breathe, yet he could not drown to be peaceful and still. White and dark images darted and screamed at him from every direction! This satanic depression lasted for days and when it ended the man who had been Wadus Strickland did not exist. That man would never live again. He knew this and realized for the first time in his life that a human being does not die all at once, but part by part, and compartment by compartment, until the door to the last room is closed and locked forever!

Wadus spoke to the stone in a low voice, "Son, I wish I had the courage to come and find you, but I do not. I will eventually come, and I will find you! I will not be able to come back here for awhile, if ever, because the place I am going will not allow it. In fact, it may allow me to come to find you much sooner. I hope it does son, I know you are not here, but rest, and know how much I love you!"

Henderson asked, "What's he saying?"

Captain Steward replied as he began to approach the kneeling man, "I can't make it out." He walked to Wadus, touched his shoulder, and said, "Strickland, there's no more time, we've gotta go." Seeing that Wadus was having trouble getting to his feet the large man put his hand under Wadus's arm and raised him to a standing position. The three men turned and made their way down the hill to the gray and black patrol unit. Neither of the men spoke or looked back toward the small white stone.

Once moving, Captain Stewart demonstrated his skill at making up for the time that had lapsed due to his detour. Spinning onto Rt. 210, he flipped on the blue flashing light, reached for the radio and reported to the station. As the dispatcher answered the Captain informed him of a "slight delay" and of their position as well as their ETA at Central Prison.

Trooper Henderson sat calmly just staring ahead as the speeding patrol unit darted around and through the heavy traffic on Interstate 40 leading to Raleigh. Henderson's disposition and manner seemed as if one man had walked up the hill to the small white stone and a different man had walked down the hill away from it. He was troubled by what he did not know and wanted to ask Captain Stewart, but he kept silent. He felt, for the first time, an imperceptible respect for the man who sat in the back seat and did not wish to add to his burden.

Wadus Strickland still showed no concern, or regret, about his destination. He did look peaceful and greatly relieved. Captain Stewart drove into Central Prison at 4:20 p.m. and was met by two correction officers. Captain Stewart went directly to the back right door and assisted the prisoner's exit. As the officers approached, Wadus Strickland's eyes looked upward into the eyes and face of Captain Stewart. Wadus started to say something but was cut off by the Captain who said, "I know Strickland, I understand! Look, you be careful in here and try to stay alive. There's nothing to be gained by dying!" Wadus slightly moved his head left to right as if to doubt the Captain's words. Captain Stewart watched momentarily as the prison officers led Wadus Strickland into Central Prison.

Captain Stewart and Trooper Henderson were headed south toward Smithfield before the silence was broken. Henderson asked, "Captain, will you please explain to me what went down this afternoon?"

The Captain did not immediately reply, looked straight ahead for a few moments and then said, "I'm not really sure I can explain, or that you could understand even if I could."

"What do you mean by that?"

"You're not married are you Henderson?"

"No I'm not."

"Do you have any children?"

"Well of course not!"

"Well son, I guess that's what I meant. Unless you had a child I'm not sure you can understand what I did this afternoon. After a slight pause he continued, "Do you remember an accident in Smithfield several months ago that resulted in the death of a young boy?"

"Yes, I do remember that."

"Well, that was the grave of that child, and that was his father we just delivered to Central Prison. This afternoon was the first time he's been to his son's grave and may well be his last. From what I know I just know I had to take him there today and I'm very glad I did. If you write it up, put that in your report!"

"What do you know about this man?"

18

"The day the accident occurred I was on my way to the station and just happened to come on it minutes later. It had not even been called in, it was that soon. Two young college students, driving under the influence, ran a stop sign at a high rate of speed and hit Strickland's vehicle. They hit him so hard his car spun around several times and then crashed into a utility pole. His son was on the side that hit the pole. The child died instantly of a broken neck. I was the first officer on the scene. I saw Strickland doing an awful job on those college boys with a baseball bat."

"That was what he was sentenced for today, right?"

"Yeah, and if I had been two seconds later, one of those would have been for murder. Strickland was just before smashing the drivers's head with that bat when I reached him. I believe one of those boys is still in the hospital. The other one is in a body cast and is scheduled for a lot of re-constructive surgery to his face."

"Damn! But I don't understand. If those guys were speeding, ran a stop sign, driving under the influence, killed a child, —why did Strickland draw twenty six years?"

"You were there today. You saw and heard what happened. You know, I've known Judge Harrison a lot of years. He's tough! But I can never remember seeing him hate to hand down a sentence like he did today."

"Why the hell wouldn't Strickland try to defend himself?"

"Who can say? Grief, guilt, shame, no will to live, who knows? Maybe it's his intention to die and he thinks Central will get the job done for him. He could be very correct!"

"What did those college guys get?"

"They haven't gone to trial yet, and probably won't."

"Why the hell not?"

"They are from very wealthy and politically connected families in Wake County. Considering the brutal beating they took from Strickland, politics, money, postponements, etc., they'll probably lose their license for some months and have to do a number of hours of community service. Watch the paper and see how far off I am. Or do you still believe everyone is equal before the law?"

"I still can't put a handle on Strickland. They claimed he was sane, and a very intelligent man. It just doesn't make any sense."

"Henderson, you're a very young man and I hope you have a good, long, and happy life in front of you, but try to remember this, life is continuous change. Nothing is constant. There are ups, downs, happy times, sad times, and there are gains and losses. We all lose things from time to time: jobs, money, houses, wives, mothers, fathers, and sometimes even a child. All of these sorrows are painful. However, the greatest loss of all, the most grievous of all, the most depressing and the most transforming of all is when a parent loses a child in death. No one can explain that loss adequately to another person."

"Captain Stewart, it sounds as though you're defending Strickland and know how he thinks."

"My only child, my son, died two years ago from leukemia. He was seventeen years old!"

Neither Captain Stewart nor Henderson spoke to each other again for the remainder of that day.

Chapter 3

Prison

"Stone walls do not a prison make, nor iron bars a cage,
Minds innocent and quiet take that for an hermitage."
Lovelace

In less than thirty minutes after Judge Harrison had sentenced Wadus Strickland, and while he was en route to Raleigh, the telephone rang in the Warden's office.

The Warden's secretary answered, "Hello, Warden White's office."

The voice at the other end spoke, "Good afternoon, this is State Senator Jacob's office calling. The Senator would like to speak with Warden White if he is available?"

"Just a moment, I'll connect you."

"Yes, this is Warden White."

State Senator Russell Jacobs began, "Good afternoon Warden White, this is State Senator Jacobs. How are you today sir?"

"Very good senator, thank you. How may I help you sir?"

"Warden White, as you probably know one of my primary objectives while in office is to reduce the crime rate in North Carolina."

"Yes sir, I have read some of your statements in the paper."

"Good, I'm pleased to hear that. I firmly believe the state must be extremely harsh in dealing with persons convicted of violent crimes. It is also my belief that until we do we will not make any progress in reversing the present trend. I have heard of the fine job you are doing at Central and would like to have more input and regular contact with you."

"Thank you senator, I will be glad to assist you in anyway possible in achieving such an objective."

"That's great Warden. I assure you I shall give you my full support at Central and if you need anything, which I'm quite sure you always do, you will not hesitate to call upon me."

"Thank you so much senator, I certainly will remember this."

"Now Warden White, I was informed a few moments ago of a man who was convicted on two counts of assault with a deadly weapon with the intent to kill. He was sentenced in Smithfield this afternoon and should be en route to Central as we speak."

"I wasn't aware of this sir. I do not know about a man until he becomes an inmate here at Central."

"Exactly Warden White, and in some cases it would be better if you did know about the crime. This is one of those cases and crimes. The man en route to Central was convicted of brutally assaulting two fine young college students with a baseball bat. These young men have been through a virtual hell of pain and suffering over the last several months. It will be years before their lives are back to normal, if ever. These young men are from fine families and they have also suffered greatly as a result of this crime."

Warden White was somewhat puzzled and replied, "That's terrible. I'm very sorry for them and their families senator."

"Yes, I'm quite sure you are. Warden White I feel we must make prison time for people who commit such crimes just as difficult as possible! I would like to set a precedent by starting with this inmate when he arrives at Central this afternoon."

Warden White hesitated but said, "Sir, I'm not quite sure I understand. I assure you that a man's life here in Central is extremely harsh and institutionalized. What exactly do you have in mind sir?"

"Well Warden, I'm sure you know the nuts and bolts better than me. However, for instance, I want this inmate in a cell with one of your most difficult and dangerous inmates. I want him to be given the most difficult, and unpleasant tasks possible and allowed few, if any, privileges. In other words Warden, I want this man's time in Central Prison to be a living hell others will not want to experience. Can I count on your support and cooperation Warden White?"

The senator's request, and tone, was so unusual that Warden White felt bewildered, intimidated, and caught somewhat off-guard. He replied reluctantly, "Well Senator Jacobs this is a very unusual request, however, if it means this much to you I'll comply with your wishes."

"Thank you Warden White, and I am very sure these fine young men, and their parents, will also be very happy to know this. Now Warden, I'm sure you understand that, for the record, this conversation has never taken place. The liberals wouldn't understand. Do you understand what I mean?"

Warden White now realized there was much here he did not know but replied, "Yes sir, I understand."

"Thank you so much Warden and I want you to know I'm in your corner and I'm in a position to help your career if you get my meaning!"

"Yes sir, I do."

"It has been a pleasure talking with you Warden and please keep me informed. Good day Warden."

"Good bye sir."

Warden White leaned back into his chair and sat staring at the black telephone as if expecting it to speak and provide him with answers to questions that troubled him. Closing his eyes and rubbing his forehead he silently thought, "I do not need this!" He felt the shame of a conspirator and wondered, "Who is this man en route. I don't know his name, his crime, his race, his record, his age, I know nothing about any of this business. I've been had! I've agreed to increase the torment of a man in a place where torment is already unbearable." He reached for the telephone and rang the receiving area.

"Hello, receiving and processing."

"Officer this is the Warden. An inmate will be arriving within the next hour. As soon as he has been processed bring him directly to my office."

The officer thought this an unusual and strange order but answered, "Yes sir, Warden."

"Oh, one more thing, don't assign this man a cell. I'll take care of that."

"Yes sir."

Wadus Strickland was led through the large intimidating doors of Central Prison to face an unseen, and unanticipated, but powerful foe that he did not know and had never seen. That serpent swam in the murky waters of the sea of politics. Yet, such demons are not always triumphant and are pitted against powerful antagonists.

Wadus Strickland had no way of knowing that his induction and processing was greatly accelerated due to his scheduled appearance before Warden White. He naturally assumed it to be standard procedure. He obediently, calmly, and without any outward display of concern followed the yellow line painted upon the floor leading from one point to the next. He was stripped, showered, given a rapid and humiliating physical, and issued oversized clothing. His number was 204. He was given soap, towel, sheet, blanket, and the standard items until the martinet routine ended. He glanced downward to the number 204 on the shirt and thought of how that number had seemed to have followed him throughout his life. It was the telephone number of his childhood home at a time when an operator requested, "Number please." It had also been his parents' postal box number. Now, here it was again. His reminiscence was brief as two corrections officers began to speed him to his unknown destination. They finally stopped in front of a door and Wadus read the words, "Warden John White." One officer knocked on the door and a commanding voice responded, "Come," and they entered.

Each of the officers held his arms as they led Wadus into the large office and to a point where he stood about four feet directly in front of his new master's desk. One of the officers stepped forward and handed the new inmate's folder to the Warden and then stepped back. Both officers stood silently behind inmate 204. Warden White had not yet looked into the face of this new inmate and directed his attention downward as he studied the file of the man standing before him. He was deliberate, and thorough, and after some time looked up directly into the face of his newest inmate. It was a cold and commanding stare of authority.

The Warden finally spoke, "Wadus Strickland, hereafter you will be known as inmate 204. Do you understand?"

"Yes."

"Yes what?"

"Yes sir."

"204 you have only two things to say while you are in Central, yes sir or no sir. Understand?"

"Yes sir."

"204 you are to serve two thirteen year terms here at Central Prison. The second term will immediately begin upon completion of the first term. As a model inmate it is possible you might cut each of these terms in half, however, I would not count on it under the State's new and stricter policies. Life here is simple, you have no decisions to make, just obey all rules, and orders, and stay out of trouble."

The Warden glanced back to the folder for a moment and said, "You just weighed in at 132 pounds. What was your weight when you entered the Johnston County jail three months ago?"

"One sixty-two sir."

Warden White leaned back in his chair and stared at the inmate for several moments before ordering, "Officers, assign inmate 204 to cell 101, which will be his new home."

Wadus could not see it but with this command each officer looked at each other as if having been slapped. One of the officers turned to face the Warden and spoke from behind Wadus.

"Warden sir, that's the cell Kabul is in!"

"So."

"But sir, no one has occupied that cell with Kabul in over three years!"

"So?"

Slightly shaking his head in obvious disbelief at this command the officer said, "Sir, I'm sure you're aware——." He was cut short by the loud and angry response from Warden White.

"Damn it officer, I don't have the time, or intention, of debating cell assignments with you! Nor do I intend to explain the orders I give you! Do you understand me officer?"

"Yes sir."

The officers led the new inmate from the Warden's office, closed the door, and looked at each other for a few silent moments. One of the officers ordered, "O.K. 204 let's move," and they led Wadus away from the Warden's office and into the cellblocks which housed the other inmates.

Warden White remained in his office for some time but did not work. He gazed downward at the file before him. He turned the pages very slowly once again in order to glean as much understanding of the day's events as possible. Finally closing the file he slowly swivelled his chair to the left, sat very still, and peered through the large windows. He looked at, but did not see, the beauty of the autumn colors in the late evening sunlight. He rose from his desk just before dusk experiencing some stomach nausea. He left his office and exited the prison gates. He had no desire for food and would have no dinner that night. He did look forward to having more than his usual two cocktails. He wondered, "Will inmate 204 be alive tomorrow morning?"

Chapter 4

The Lion

*"Every man is a volume, if you
know how to read him."* William E. Channing

As the two officers escorted the new inmate to his cell they paused momentarily and one motioned to two other officers standing some distance away. As they approached, the officer said, "You guys come with us to take 204 to his cell."

One of the summoned officers looked Wadus over and asked, "You need help with this inmate?"

"We're taking him to cell 101."

"Oh W-e-l-l, now that's different."

The four officers stopped in front of cell 101 and one of them shouted, "Open 101," and the door opened with a loud clang. Wadus was pushed into the cell and all four officers entered behind him.

As Wadus stood holding all of his prison issue he saw a man kneeling, with his head to the floor, in the rear of the cell. The man looked up as if surprised and began to rise.

An officer spoke quickly with authority, "Stay back where you are Kabul!" Another officer removed the iron from the wrist of the inmate. All four officers were very alert and directed all of their attention to the man at the rear of the cell.

Wadus stood in total awe as he watched the colossal figure come to his knees and slowly stand to face the intruders.

27

Wadus began to take inventory of what was possibly one of the largest and most powerful appearing humans he had ever viewed. For a moment he forgot about being in prison as he was so captivated by what he saw. It seemed as if a giant tree was maturing very rapidly right in front of where he stood.

The man was black, very black, and was at least six feet, six inches tall. He weighed three hundred pounds if not more. It was obvious he had made much use of the prison gym. There was no cellulose on this body! His arms and chest stretched every tread of the shirt he wore as if the slightest movement would result in a rip. Wadus was so stunned by this immense figure, compared to his own diminutive size, his first thought was of how David must have felt when he stood before Goliath! He further thought, "I don't even have a sling shot!"

The huge man spoke loudly as he stepped forward, "What da hell yo bringin dis white ass cracker in my house fo? Yo knows I don't hav no house gues in my home! Specially whittie!"

"You do now Kabul, so just back up and nobody will get hurt." The officers backed out of the cell and the door closed with a loud bang. The giant came quickly past Wadus and began shouting to the officers as they walked away.

"Hey man, git yor sorry white asses back here. I don't stand fo shit lik dis!" They did not acknowledge his protest and were soon out of sight.

As the officers left the area one of them said, "We might as well have gone ahead and put that man on death row."

"Yeah, but then this way will probably be a lot quicker. I just can't figure why the Warden did this. How long do you give this inmate? Maybe we should start a pool or something?"

"Well, I don't think he'll cost the state very much, that's for damn sure."

The giant whirled, looked down at Wadus, and brought both huge fists up so quickly and powerfully that everything Wadus held went in many different directions. Wadus stood very still and looked up as the prodigious figure slightly pressed against him. The giant spoke with great anger, "White boy, why da fuck yo in my house, I ain't had no cellmate in mo dan three years?"

"The Warden didn't give me much selection." The power source immediately struck Wadus in the chest with both fists and great force. Wadus's body was propelled against the back wall and he slid to the floor. He was quickly lifted from the floor and slammed again against the wall. The giant suddenly released Wadus and again he met the floor. His vision was blurred; his body ached and became increasingly feeble. He watched as the giant bent down, picked up a small rug, folded it neatly and placed it on a small table. Once again the giant returned to his victim, once again Wadus was snatched upward and smashed violently into the wall several more times. Wadus thought of his son and remembered thinking this place might allow him to go to his Jamie very soon.

The giant asked in a deep growl, "What da hell yo gotta say now yo white ass sodie cracker?"

Without expressing the pain his body was experiencing Wadus looked into the fierce dark eyes of the giant and whispered, "You were kneeling in the wrong direction."

"Say what," bellowed the giant as he once again threw his victim against the sidewall and watched as he wilted to the floor once again. The giant approached again and stood looking down. "What da hell yo means, da wrong direction?"

Wadus hesitated but weakly replied, "Your prayer rug wasn't facing Mecca."

The giant bent down, looked Wadus in the face, and asked, "An jus what da hell yo know bout ah prayer rug yo white ass racist southern Baptist asshole?"

"I know the directions of a compass and Mecca isn't in the direction you were praying!"

The giant stood up quickly and announced, "Man my name is Mohamet Kabul, I is ah Black Muslim an I hates whites!"

With his eyes almost closed Wadus asked, "What's the difference between a black Muslim and a white Muslim?"

The giant bent down and quickly grabbed his victim tightly around the throat and said, "Man, if yos makin ah white ass joke bout me I gonna crush yo skinny ass neck!"

Gathering enough wind to whisper, Wadus said, "I just thought all Muslims followed the same Pillars of Islam."

The giant released his grip and stared momentarily then asked, "If yos knows so damn much, what is da five Pillars of Islam?"

With his eyes closed Wadus began to recite the five Pillars of the Islamic Faith. "The first is, There is no God but Allah and Mohammed is his Prophet. The second is, one must pray five times each day facing the Holy City of Mecca. The third, one must give alms to the poor and needy. The fourth, one must fast during the Holy Month of Ramadan. The last is, one must make a pilgrimage to the Holy City of Mecca at least once during his lifetime. I just thought all Muslims, regardless of race, followed the same ones."

The giant rose slowly, walked to the front of the cell, and stood looking out through the bars. Without turning he asked, "Which is da right direction to Mecca from dis cell?"

"It's east or west, but closer if facing east. You were kneeling and facing to the south."

"Yo shore bout dat!"

"Yes."

"Man, yo damn well better be!" He turned and walked slowly to the bed and lay down on the bottom bunk. Wadus remained where he sat on the floor.

Mohamet Kabul was the alpha male of Central Prison and this status was recognized by officers and inmates alike. Whites, blacks, and all others stepped aside for this man. He was like a lion with no peers. Yet, even the lion must protect himself from the flies. Wadus Strickland was to become his fly. The lamb had been thrown to the lion but the lion would have no appetite for his intended morsel!

Wadus tried but could not move from where he sat. He had not eaten since early morning. With the events of the day and the pounding he had just taken the strength just was not in him to move. He was not hungry for over the past several months of depression food had not appealed to his palate. He suspected he was becoming anorexic. He longed for the peace of deep sleep even if it was to be an eternal sleep. He was semi-conscious but heard the deep voice of Mohamet.

"Man, yo say da Warden done put yo in dis cell, he don't do dat shit! Dat's some white ass honkie screws' job ta sign cells!"

"Well, he's the one who put me in this one, he said cell 101 and this is where the officers brought me."

Mohamet sat up quickly on the side of his bunk, faced Wadus, and said; "If dat's true somebody out dey wants yo white ass dead, bad dead!"

"You could be right," and he began to understand his had not been a normal induction procedure and further he had been assigned to a cell where no other inmate had been allowed for over three years.

"Mother fucker, yo got some heavy duty bad ass enemies on da other side of dees walls man. M-o-t-h-e-r F-u-c-k! What in da shit did yo do outside an who da hell did yo do it to?"

Wadus heard the question but could not generate the energy for the explanation Mohamet wanted and only replied, "Allah Akbar. God's will be done." These words seemed to silence the lion and he lay back upon his bunk once again. Wadus tried once again to get to his feet but could not. The strength was not available. He leaned over and lay upon the floor.

His eyes closed as he drifted into a dream world of semi sleep accompanied by flashback memories of his childhood in Robeson County, North Carolina during the forties and fifties. He saw his brother and could hear the laughter as they ran barefoot on blistering sandy roads often feeling the pain of sandspurs. He saw the milk cows, chickens, hogs, and the gigantic garden that had occupied much of their time. Here they had learned to work, to be responsible, and to be obedient. He saw "Blackie," their huge, powerful, and fierce yard dog who had provided them and the home place with total security. The physical and mental agony he felt was soothed by the closeness they shared as a result of poverty. These memories subdued his pain and he thought there is, even with all of its deprivations, an aesthetic quality nurtured by the simplicity of poverty. He felt as though he had been blessed rather than deprived.

At first he thought it was part of his dream but realized he was being lifted from the floor. With slight effort the lion took him over and quickly tossed him onto the bare mattress of the top bunk, as a large cat would flip a mouse into the air. Wadus heard words but was not conscious enough to understand them. He remembered nothing more of his first night in cell 101.

Chapter 5

The Key
*"The pain of the mind is worse
than the pain of the body."* Syrus

Mohmaet Kabul, the alpha male, Goliath, the lion, of
Central Prison was thirty-four years old. He had been
in prison since he was twenty-five after having been
sentenced to thirty-five years. He had argued with two white
men, and when attacked, had killed one of them with a single
blow to the man's temple. Society had prepared the crime but
he had committed it and like so many thousands of his race and
economic status he had not been able to afford the enormous
expense of acquiring true justice. During his nine years at
Central Prison his sentence had been increased due to a number
of violent confrontations with officers as well as inmates. On
the surface he appeared to be an introvert and his many trips to
solitary confinement seemed to bother him little and had done
nothing to modify his behavior or break his spirit.

He had grown up in rural Wayne County, North Carolina.
His father was a tenant farmer, there were nine children, and
Mohamet had only been allowed to reach the seventh grade. He
had not been allowed the luxury of adolescence and was forced
to leap from childhood to manhood by necessity. His labors
had always been manual, hard, and his rewards almost non-
existent. It was as though, "he dug a ditch, to earn the money,
to buy the bread, to give him the strength, to dig a ditch." He
did become strong and had greatly increased that power during

his years in Central. His fearful status in this institution was all he had to be proud of and he protected that status.

Wadus Strickland, inmate 204, was ignorant of his cellmates' past, his reputation, and how he had been stereotyped by everyone in this dismal environment. He had not had any contact with anyone else and was not aware that no one expected his life expectancy to be more than a few days. Wadus was to learn to use Jeanne Roland's advice, "the feeble tremble before opinion, the foolish defy it, the wise judge it, the skillful direct it." He did not tremble because he did not know Mohamet's reputation or record. Neither did he judge it for the same reason. He was not foolish enough to defy what he saw, but he was skillful enough to eventually direct it and to use it as a shield.

Wadus awoke the following morning to face his first day in prison and a new world from which he would probably never emerge. At first he thought he was still in the Johnston County jail, however as he forced himself to sit upright, he realized this was not the case. There was the sound of loud voices, clanging metal, his head throbbed, his face was swollen, and his arms and chest ached.

He heard the deep voice of the giant, "Git down cracker, dey takin us ta eat."

Wadus attempted to do as told but went down to the floor. Glancing down Mohamet snatched him erect with one hand and said, "Dis fuckin sucks, I hates yo white lint head ass!"

Almost as a tutorial conditioned reflex Wadus asked, "Why" as he looked at Mohamet.

Mohamet quickly punched him in the forehead with one finger and said, "Fuck you! Stay way from me man!"

As Mohamet was stepping out of the cell Wadus said, "You really like that "f" word don't you." He received a quick angry look as Mohamet exited cell 101. The line of inmates had stopped to allow the big man to go ahead but had no intention of allowing inmate 204 the same opportunity. Wadus finally took his position as the last in line. He did not mind, however, as this allowed him to move slowly and with less pain. As the inmates had passed each silently looked him over completely. Wadus could sense their keen interest and apparent surprise. They seemed to be amazed to see him still alive.

The cafeteria was large, crowded, and noisy. Wadus finally approached the serving area and watched what was to be breakfast slammed onto his tray. The workers made gestures and comments concerning him as he was served. After passing through the serving line he looked all around for a place to sit and finally saw a table with quite a lot of empty space. He made his way to the table and sat down. He glanced over and saw Mohamet a little further down on the other side of the table. No one other than himself was close by.

"Whittie, yo at da wrong table! Nobody sits here, specially you!"

"There's no place else to sit."

"Yo ass is dead mother fucker!"

"Allah's' will be done."

Mohamet slammed his tray onto the table, stood up, took his tray to the disposal area and went to wait to be returned to his cell. Wadus rapidly forced down the food even though he thought it might come back up. He realized how weak he was and how much his body needed food, even this food. After the meal all inmates were taken back to their cells.

Mohamet was waiting when Wadus stepped into cell 101. Standing with his hands on his hips it was clear he was extremely angry. He stuck out his arm and pointed to Wadus but before he could pronounce his judgment Wadus said, "Yes, I know, I understand. I know you can and will kill me. I also know I really don't care and would not try to stop you. No point in trying anyway. So, go ahead, kill me big man. You'll be doing me a favor, one I don't have the guts to do for myself. I don't fear it, I rather look forward to it. But remember this big man, a very wise person once said, 'he who conquers others is strong, he who conquers himself is mighty.' Yes, you're a strong man but you're not mighty, even though you could be."

Mohamet was obviously caught off guard and said, "Yo skinny white ass talks a bunch ah bullshit."

"Well, maybe, but think about this. I am not your enemy. Why am I in your house? You said last night someone wants me dead, or to suffer a great deal. You are supposed to, and expected to, kill me. So, let them use you like some mindless dummy the way others have probably always used you. Or, you can think for yourself. I don't know all of the precise details, but what I've said is obvious and very true. You hate me cause my skin is white and yours is black. Well, what color is your soul, is it black also? The shade of the skin is not important but the color of a person's soul is! Now, you have a decision to make."

"Oh yeah, what's dat white boy?"

"You can kill me, as they want you to, you can let others use and control you, or you can be in control and think for yourself. You can be a man in control of himself, thinking for himself, and refusing to be someone's fool and fall guy."

Mohamet stood silently and stared at his skinny white cellmate. He was obviously thinking seriously about what he had just heard.

Wadus took advantage of this and said, "I don't know how long you have been a prisoner behind these walls, but don't ever let anyone put walls and bars around your mind. No one can do that unless your allow them to do it."

Mohamet slowly sat down at the table and gazed at an old copy of the Koran for a moment and then asked, "Man, what's yo name?"

"Wadus Strickland."

"Wadus! I ain't never heard ah name lik dat. Wadus— some name." Looking up at Wadus he asked, "yo shore bout dat way ta face Mecca?"

"Yes, I am."

Mohamet took the small rug from the table, stood and said, "Show me, cause hits time to pray."

Wadus instructed him as to the direction of the east and watched as this giant of a man put his knees and head to the floor and prayed.

When Mohamet had finished and the rug carefully folded and put away he turned to Wadus and inquired, "What religion is you?"

Wadus slightly shook his head and thought seriously about this serious question and then replied, "I think I'm part of many different religions."

"What's dat suppose ta mean?"

"Well, you were right last night about me being a Southern Baptist because that's the way I was reared in Robeson County.

But over the last thirty years I have studied, and taught about, all of the world's major religions. Basically, they all teach the same precepts. I believe, and know, there is absolutely one universal God. I also know that only before Him are all people equal. Semantics, names, geography, politics, greed, and a host of other factors have made it impossible for different faiths to see and understand this fact. Can you imagine how the wars would rage in the Heavens if there were a different God for each religion? They would have done to the universe what man has often done to the earth. No, there is only one God, regardless of the name He is known by. I happen to worship as a Christian but I am quite certain God shows no more love for me than He does for people of other lands and faiths. He would not be God otherwise would he?"

"I become a Muslim when I got in here. Ah old man taught me, he giv me dis Book. He's dead now. I tries but I don't read so good an don't know a bunch of dem big words. Does yo believe in Allah?"

"Allah is the Arabic word for God. Yes, I believe in Allah."

"Yo talks lik ah educated man, what did yo do fo ah livin?"

"I was a school teacher."

"Is dat right. I didn't git much schoolin, an what I did git dey weren't much ta it. I had ta go ta work in da fields when I was thirteen year old ta hep feed da family. I wish I'd learnt mo when I wuz dey but den I didn't thank much bout hit. I shore has since."

"Would you like to learn? I have lots of time now to teach you and it would be like having your own private tutor. You have lots of time too and can learn whatever you really wish to learn."

Mohamet's head snapped upward and Wadus Strickland knew he had touched upon a great psychological need and desire within this powerful yet weak man. He thought, "If only I could be skillful enough to direct such physical power, and energy, properly and in the right direction—what could it really become?"

Mohamet replied, "I think bout hit."

37

Wadus sat down against the wall and realized that for the first time since June his mind, and thoughts, had been for someone other than his Jamie. He felt somewhat guilty but experienced an emotion common to the joy he had known and loved when a classroom teacher instructing young people. He also felt quite safe now and did not fear the great strength of this giant with whom he was to share a cell.

Wadus Strickland's tormentors, unknown and unseen by him, had actually placed him where he was to have the greatest amount of security in this very dangerous environment. Other inmates would quickly assume him to be the property of the most feared man within their world. Only once would any dare to challenge that assumption of ownership. Wadus had heard, and read, of the many sexual horrors which new inmates often experience and admitted that it was the only aspect of his new world that truly frightened him. He thought of being forced into sexual contact with another male and believed such degradation might well give him the incentive to do what he did not now have the courage to do. Wadus had correctly calculated Mohamet to be heterosexual and this also provided a great sense of relief. Now, if he could only study his subject enough to accurately know how, and when, to unlock the door of the great façade he had created about himself through fear and intimidation.

Chapter 6

The Black Angel

*"ofttimes the test of courage becomes
rather to live than to die."* Alfieri

Warden White arrived at Central Prison earlier than usual the following morning. He had not had any dinner the previous evening and a number of cocktails. He had not rested well yet felt an unusual desire to get to his office at Central as soon as possible. He needed to know what had occurred overnight behind those walls and his conscience prayed for good news.

He entered his office, did not ask for his usual coffee, and went immediately to his desk and began to study the details of the events recorded in the nightly log. He leaned back into his chair and breathed a deep sigh of relief. There was no record of any unusual activity, or death, recorded. He buzzed his secretary, "Have Sergeant Johnson report to my office please." His order was followed and the sergeant was soon in his office.

"Good morning Sergeant."

"Good morning Warden."

"I'm curious about inmate 204 who arrived late yesterday. What is his status this morning?"

"Sir, I just checked on him about thirty minutes ago when I learned some dummy downstairs had assigned him to cell 101."

"I was that dummy Sergeant."

The Sergeant was embarrassed and shocked, "Oh—I'm sorry sir, it's just that is the cell of Mohamet Kabul and he has been alone for over three years."

"Well, we can't afford private cells any longer. How is inmate 204?"

"Sir I went to see for myself and although he looked pretty bad he was better than I expected him to be."

"How did he look?"

"His face was swollen and bruised, and he seemed to be in quite a lot of pain. I asked him what had happened and he said he had fallen from the upper bunk during the night. He must have fallen a number of times to get in the condition I observed."

"Yeah, right. Have the infirmary check him."

"Yes sir, I will."

"Well as soon as he's able assign him to a work detail and keep me up to date on his status. That's all Sergeant."

"Yes sir." The sergeant left the Warden's office and returned to his duties.

Warden White felt better, and more relieved, than he had since receiving Senator Jacob's call. It had occurred to him during the past troubling night that he was indeed the Warden of Central Prison and not Senator Jacobs. Jacobs would not be there to know what was happening to inmate 204. He would not treat 204 differently than any other inmate, yet would tell the good senator what he wanted to hear. Once again he pulled the new inmate's folder from his desk and studied it carefully once more before having the secretary file it. He did not know why but sensed something about the man that had stood before him the day before and the man's record enhanced that sensation. He knew in his mind, and heart, that inmate 204 was not a criminal!

Each day of the next year was an adventure with an uncertain ending for Wadus Strickland. There were dangerous times and exhausting hours of labor, but at all times he kept his objective clearly in focus. He would only allow himself to remember his beautiful son, the large field, and the small stone where he rested. He felt no hatred for the young men responsible for his son's death but was not at all sorry for what he had done to them. Almost everyone, and everything, he had experienced before that dreadful June afternoon had no meaning. This mental state enabled him to suppress the emotional agony most inmates endure during confinement. Outside of cell 101 he said only, "Yes sir" or "No sir" and did whatever he was told to do. He was assigned to a cleaning detail and spent his days mopping and scrubbing all floors.

Three weeks after he had begun his cleaning assignment he was mopping and cleaning urinals in one of the smaller first level restrooms. Four white men entered. The last one closed the door and leaned his large frame against it. It was obvious no one else was to be allowed to enter. Wadus stood silently as the other three men started toward him. He rolled bucket and mop with him as he backed against the far wall. The men stopped momentarily, smiled at each other, and looked amusingly at him.

First Inmate: "Men this puny bastard is Kabuls' bitch!"

Second Inmate: "Th only thing I hate worse than ah nigger is a white nigger fucker!"

Third Inmate: "Now nigger fucker, we gonna give you some white meat to compare with that black snake of Kabul!"

All three laughed as they moved quickly forward grabbing Wadus and slapping him back and forth. Each took rapid turns at this and then turned him around and smashed his face into the tile wall.

Wadus wanted to plead, scream, pass out, and most of all prayed to die suddenly of heart failure as he felt he might. He could do none of these and realized he was about to descend into the hell of prison, which he feared the most. Two men held his body securely against the wall as the other man jerked down Wadus's trousers. They all laughed and joked.

"This is gonna be the skinniest piece of ass I've ever had." He began to lower the shorts Wadus wore. Wadus tried to remember every psychological technique he had ever taught in order to help him endure what he was experiencing. Suddenly there was a tremendous bang! The door flew open as if hit by a locomotive and sending the man against it smashing into the opposite wall. Mohamet Kabul stepped slowly into the restroom, closed the door, and faced the four white inmates who had quickly grouped together. Wadus turned his head from the wall and looked at Mohamet. Once again he was absolutely sure there was a God in Heaven and at this very moment His strong right hand had just entered this prison restroom.

Mohamet stood silently. His enormous body began to flinch and come to an accelerated new pace. His chest, and arms, swelled and tightened. His jaw muscles danced as if experiencing an electrical shock. Wadus was astounded. He knew his cellmate was powerful but this went way beyond what he dreamed a body was capable of becoming. It seemed as though there had been another Mohamet even more powerful hiding inside of the outward Mohamet. The four white men were definitely afraid but seemed to feel safe with the four to one odds. Mohamet did not move and glared violently as if black lightening might flash from his eyes at any moment!

"Hey, what's happin Kabul?" There was no reply and he continued, "We just thought we might have a little fun with this new meat here." Mohamet took a slow step forward and the man quickly extended his arm pointing and said, "O.K. man, no problem. You want him, he's all yours. We'll git outta here and you can have your fun with him." It was clear to all four men that their exit would be much more difficult than their entry had been. Suddenly they lunged toward their opponent. Wadus watched Mohamet's movements and felt he was viewing the masterful, and intricate, strokes of an orchestra conductor and hearing the sounds of several violent storms all at once.

Mohamet struck the first man in the face with such force he landed on the floor next to where Wadus stood. He was still and bleeding. He then grabbed the next man with a lightening throat hold and used his body as a shield and ram against the other two men. His other large fist struck again, again, and again, until the two men were on the floor in obvious pain. Mohamet looked at the man he held by the throat. Looking directly into the man's eyes he applied greater and greater pressure until the man's arms dropped to his sides. He too was silent and still. Mohamet hurled him with great force, head first, into the tile wall. He lay unconscious upon the floor. Mohamet quickly refocused and began with the others. He struck them rapidly until both were bleeding badly and were unconscious. Wadus stood spellbound as if he was witnessing the dawn of creation, or either its final moments. He had not even pulled up his trousers and held onto the mop handle as if it were the staff of Moses.

Mohamet directed his attention toward Wadus and looked him up and down and said, "Man yo look so fuckin stupid! An yo is stupid! Git yo puny white ass outta here. NOW!"

Wadus quickly obeyed, jerked up his trousers, and then guided the bucket using the mop handle made a rapid exit into the hallway. He hesitated some distance down the hall, looked back, and saw Mohamet slowly and calmly exit the restroom. He casually walked away in the opposite direction.

Wadus realized his free hand was trembling. Everything had happened with such speed, violence, and unbelievable results his mind could not yet comprehend all he had witnessed. He continued to watch Mohamet and was quite certain he was viewing a black angel disappear down the hallway.

Wadus began to slowly mop his way down the wide hallway. It was only minutes before he heard the shrill whistle of alarm. Several officers rushed toward the direction of the restroom and a crowd of inmates began to gather. A few moments later the four badly injured men who were found in the restroom were rushed to the prison infirmary. They would spend a number of days there before healing enough to be returned to their cells. As is the code among all inmates neither would tell the officers how they all came to be there in that condition. Their story was that they were attacked from behind by a number of black inmates but did not have a chance to see who they were. By the evening mealtime the true account of what had occurred was common knowledge among most of the inmates in Central Prison.

Wadus now had a much better understanding of why Mohamet was so feared by his peers and officers alike. Why he ate alone, why he had had a cell alone, and why he now had more years to serve than when he had arrived. He also felt he knew much more about what was behind his cellmate's massive forehead and not visible. His loneliness, the self-imposed isolation from companions, being the beast others feared, being a prisoner in his own mind due to a lack of education, were none of this man's innermost subconscious desires.

Most of the other inmates were already at their tables as Wadus walked to Mohamet's table for the last meal of that day. He realized almost every man in the room watched as he took his seat across the table. He sat for a moment and stared at the giant and started to speak. Mohamet looked sternly and spoke first, "Shut up! We talk later." He then again shocked Wadus by taking his own carton of milk and placing in on Wadus's tray. He said, "Drink dat, yo best put some meat on dat skinny white ass." As they finished the meal he instructed Wadus to, "Take dis tray an put hit up."

"What?"

"Jes do hit man." Wadus did as told and most of the other inmates watched and mumbled.

Once back in cell 101 both men sat and stared at each other for several moments. Wadus was certain he was about to be thoroughly verbally chastised. But before either could say anything an officer appeared at the door and it opened with the usual loud metal clang. He walked to where Mohamet sat and looking down asked, "Kabul, how did you get all that skin knocked off your knuckles?"

Mohamet did not look up and replied, "I fell on somethin."

"Yeah, I think I saw what you fell on earlier this afternoon." The officer left the cell and the door closed behind him.

Mohamet turned and casually said, "I been thinkin bout what yo said some weeks back. Yo wuz ah teacher, yo thinks yo can learn me ta read better?"

Wadus was elated but tried not to over react and replied, "No doubt about it, I certainly can."

"Well, I tells yo what I is cided ta do. I is gonna try ta keep yo puny ass alive in here, an I gonna try to learn yo how ta maybe hep keep yoself alive. Yo wuz damn lucky dis afternoon, da right brother jes happin ta see dat white cracker trash foller yo ass in dat toilet an he got da word ta me fast. Man, yos got ta watch ever move ya makes, all da time, an what's happin all round ya, in ever direction, all da time. Yo ain't gat nough meat on yo ass ta take a blade an live. Fool, dis

44

ain't no damn hi school classroom. Man, yo diggin what I is sayin ta ya?"

"Yes."

"Yo acts lik ya wants somebody ta kills ya. Now, after taday all of'em gonna thank yo my lady. Dats good, an I don't care cause I ain't dat way, but no body gonna try dat wit ya agin. Dat is less some of'em kills me fust, an deys some blacks an a whole bunch of whites dat wants ta do jes dat. So when I tells ya to do sumthin ya does it quick, ya foller close ta me in da yard, or where ever we is."

"Is this why you gave me your milk tonight?"

"Yeah, dats one of da reasons. Sides, I been ah throwin hit in da trash anyways. Blacks can't handle drinkin too much milk anyhows. Yo otta know dat if yo wuz ah school teacher. Now, I gonna do dees thangs fo yo an yo gonna learn me better. We do dis some ever night right here in dis cell, O.K.?"

"Yes, I understand, you've got a deal!" He extended his open right hand toward Mohamet. Mohamet looked surprised and reacted shyly as if experiencing something for the first time. It may have well been the first time a white man had ever extended his hand in friendship to this man. Mohamet wrapped his monstrous hand around Wadus's hand and they shook. A deal had been struck. Wadus would be protected from the perversion he feared most and he would teach this giant as payment.

Wadus thought of the day's events as he tried to force himself to sleep. But his mind was too charged for sleep. He thought of his Jamie, the little stone, the big field, and his heart ached to be with his son. He remembered his childhood in Robeson County and again thought of the giant, fierce, yard dog they simply called "Blackie." He remembered how Blackie had hated the chickens they raised, but how he had been taught not to harm them and how he would flee when the chickens were turned out to forage in the open spaces of the home place. He would never forget how astonished, and bewildered, all had been when this hater of chickens had chosen to protect one single cripple chicken from being pecked to death by the healthy ones. He could still see Blackie, with his head held back as if to avoid the unpleasantness of his duty, standing over the cripple. Blackie raced to the cripple chicken's rescue daily and the cripple lived a long time as another yard pet. Wadus now understood how that crippled chicken must have felt and wondered if some higher power had been trying to teach him an important lesson early in life. These pictures were as a sedative to Wadus and he slept.

The good Senator Jacobs would never know he had not only saved this inmate's life but had given him an incentive to live, or at least to court death less passionately?

Chapter 7

Classroom 101
"You cannot teach a man anything; you can only help him to find it within himself." Galileo

Mohamet had accurately predicted what all inmates would assume about their relationship. Wadus followed his mentor's instructions when they were not in lockup and day by day further reinforced the stereotype charade by which he was perceived. The impressions others inside of these walls had of him had no impact or meaning. Neither was he concerned about what minds on the other side of the walls would think, or say, about him. The world he had known had never loved, or been kind, to him. He did not miss it, or wish to return to it, for he had not loved that world either.

Wadus Strickland was totally aware of his complete metamorphosis and concentrated upon a metaphysical world where he longed to be. What others thought of him would not make him a better, or worse, human being. What he was he had become during the days and nights of nightmares following the accident. Something had touched him, had changed his entire being, and he sensed an awareness of things people are not supposed to be aware of. He had stepped across some cosmic threshold but had not been allowed to remain. He did not understand it, but knew he felt nearer to self-actualization than ever before. He enjoyed an inner calmness, and acceptance without judgment, of all things. He was the former Wadus Strickland only in appearance.

Mohamet tutored him by day and he instructed Mohamet by night. Over the days, weeks, and months of the coming year both made great progress in their perspective schools. It took Wadus some time, and great patience, to strip Mohamet of the façade by which he had disguised himself for many years. Wadus discovered a completely different human entity. He became as a giant sponge attempting to absorb all mental moisture possible. The first several weeks were burned-up with nights of questions, riddles, discussions, and stories of some of the great figures of history. Wadus had to first determine the capabilities of his student before deciding reasonable objectives and how best to proceed.

The first night they began Wadus asked, "Mohamet, have you ever heard of a man known as Socrates?"

"No."

"He is said to have been one of the greatest teachers who ever lived. He lived in ancient Greece and taught by asking questions which made his students think. His motto was, "Know Thyself.""

"What da fuck do dat mean? Everbody knows who dey is. I is Mohamet Kabul. Man dats dumb."

"I want you to stop using that "F" word so much. I'll show you some better ones that mean the same thing."

"It's jus ah word I uses, I don't even thank bout hit."

"Yes, I understand but when someone uses that word a lot it sends messages and says something else about them."

"Lik what?"

"Like the person doesn't know how to express himself using good vocabulary or words. Many people have that same problem. Now, Socrates also said, "People do not like to think because thinking is hard work.""

"Thinkin is work. Man, I is done a lot of hard work an thinkin ain't no work."

"Thinking can be very hard work. Sometimes it even drives persons insane. It takes thinking to figure out problems, to search for reasons, and to find true and accurate answers. For instance, you have probably heard someone say, "I'm worried to death over such and such, or I'm so worried about this that I'm sick on my stomach, or have a terrible headache." What he is really saying is that he has a problem, or situation, he can't think through and deal with. When he finds the answer all of a sudden the worry, aches, and pains go away and he feels real good. Yes, thinking can be tough and you must think long, and hard, about yourself before you can truly understand and know yourself. Many people never do, but if you can come to really know yourself you will then be in control of your own life. No one can use you, no one can control you, inside or outside of these walls. Now let's try a little thinking exercise. There is a Russian proverb which states, "Fat bears are no match for lean wolves," now think about that and tell me what you think it means."

Mohamet appeared uneasy and off guard but nodded his large head. Wadus felt it might well be the first time anyone had ever asked this man to think and to give his opinion on anything.

"Dat means dem wolves is thin cause dey hungry and ain't had much ta eat. Den dey gits mean and sneaky. Dat bear probably lazy an ain't in no good shape. Dey watch dat fat bear and slips up on'em foe he knows hit. Dem wolves gonna git his fat lazy ass."

Wadus clapped his hands together, looked at Mohamet and said, "That's terrific, excellent, bulls eye on the first shot." Mohamet smiled broadly and was very pleased with himself and the recognition he received.

"Now, how can you apply what you just said to life, people, and the world?"

"Dat's lik when I wuz on da outside, even dem years I went ta dat school, I knowed younguns and grown folks dat had way mo dan dey needed an didn't never have ta work fo any of hit. Ever thang wuz give to'em. But dey wuz weak and couldn't take care of demselves. I didn't think much of'em."

"You didn't respect them?"

"Dat's right, I didn't."

"That's very, very good. Mohamet, you know and understand much more than you realize. Your reasoning capacity is excellent. Now, I want you to be like one of those lean and hungry wolves with what we are going to begin to learn. Don't get discouraged, we've got lots of time."

There were to be hundreds of hours of discussions, questions, instruction and mental exchanges between these two men in the coming year. Wadus always encouraged his student to think and to discover the answer for himself. He slowly increased the difficulty of objectives, and the student met the challenge.

Wadus began with phonics. Mohamet slowly, but definitely, learned to enunciate the sound of each letter of the alphabet. His mentor praised each small success and delighted the student. Wadus had seldom beheld such pride, and joy, as when Mohamet tackled and mastered his first "big word" using the phonics he had learned. The dictionary became Mohamet's favorite book, next to his Koran, and Wadus did introduce substitutes for four letter words. Mohamet found this very amusing. It became more and more difficult for Wadus to bring the nightly exercises to a conclusion. The bond between teacher and student became stronger day by day and Mohamet became more and more conscientious in his duties as protector of inmate 204.

Mohamet made great progress and after a year read slowly but quite well. He had learned to pronounce most of his conversational vocabulary properly when he concentrated on breaking old habits. He used the "f" word less and less, "dis" became "this", "dey" became "they," "dem" became "them," "dat" became "that," and on and on. Wadus was probably happier with Mohamet's achievements than he was himself.

Neither man had ever spoken much of the outside, freedom, or the possibility of ever experiencing either again. Wadus's ex-wife had come to the prison once but when he refused to see her she never returned. One evening he sat in the small chair in the cell as he stared at a letter he held. After sometime he rose, tore it into small pieces, walked over and flushed it down the toilet.

Mohamet watched with great interest and said, "You didn't even open that. Do you know who it was from?"

"Yes, my ex-wife."

"Do you hate her that much?"

"No, not at all. The man she wrote that letter to died over a year ago. I don't want to read a dead man's mail."

"Wadus, you're getting crazy on me again, man. Sometimes you scare me man, I feel like I'm in this cell with some kind of ghost or something. Besides, what if there was money in that envelope?"

"I don't need it, all my bills here are paid by the state."

Mohamet did not understand his cellmate but sensed his questions tormented him and did not ask any others.

Later that night as they lay in the darkness Wadus asked in a low curious tone, "Mohamet, have you ever been married?"

"No."

"Do you have any children?"

"No, but I had a lady and was almost ready to start a family when I got into that mess with those white guys. You know Wadus, since I've learned some things I wish I had just let those rednecks beat me up. I'd be with my lady now and probably have some children. You have any children Wadus?"

"I had a son. He died."

"Yeah, I've heard some stories about it. That's why you're in here ain't it?"

"Isn't it."

"Screw you honkie."

"Well, that's better than the "f" word anyway. Good night."

Neither man spoke again that night but Wadus took a long mental trip into his past. He thought of the good years of his marriage. He remembered the depression he had gone through when he discovered she was unfaithful. Yet he did not hate her for his was a story told, and retold, thousands of times each day across the land. He knew no one ever really owns anyone else and the greatest gift you can bestow upon a human being is the gift of freedom to go if so desired. He did hate every minute he had been deprived of his son's companionship. He hated the fact that he had not had sex for over four years. Most of all he hated thinking of the possibility his son might still be alive if things had been different. He hated himself for not dying on that June afternoon with his Jamie.

Wadus had one other visitor that first year. Five months after his arrival at Central he was informed of a man who had come to visit him. He could not imagine who, or his purpose, so agreed to see the visitor and was escorted to the visitation area. The officer pointed to a table where a rather large man sat. As Wadus approached and sat down he was shocked to recognize Captain Stewart who had driven him to Central from Smithfield.

"Hello Captain."

"Hello Strickland, you look much better than when I last saw you."

"Well, I've been staying in a lot at night, eating, sleeping, and working on a pretty routine schedule. I guess that's good for one's metabolism."

"I just decided to stop by and see how you were doing. Having any major problems?"

"No sir, not really. Captain, I've thought about what you did for me on the way here, I don't know why you did it, but I want you to know how grateful I am."

"No problem, forget about it. Is there anything I can do for you on the outside?"

"No sir, but thank you anyway. By the way Captain, how's that young trooper doing who was with you that day?"

"Trooper Henderson, oh he's good. I think he's actually growing up and will make a fine officer. Well, I've gotta go so take care of yourself and try to shorten your sentence as much as possible."

"Yes sir, good bye and thank you for coming Captain."

The visit had been brief. Wadus was puzzled and questioned the "why" of it? He did not know of the Captain's son dying of leukemia. Nor did he know that every Saturday the Captain faithfully visited his son's grave. He did not know how much emotional pain and endless grief they shared.

The days, weeks, and months, of the first year were mostly one day's experience repeated three hundred and sixty-five times. Wadus continued his cleaning chores during the day and instruction of Mohamet each night. The student was now at a point he could read well, use the limited library, and needed to rely on Wadus less and less. Wadus mostly listened, occasionally questioning and correcting. He felt a tremendous sense of accomplishment and was proud of the different man Mohamet was becoming. Mohamet's physical superiority continued to go unchallenged, yet he was much more calm and had less and less confrontations with other inmates as well as officers. This was especially noticed by the officers who had been called upon in past years to subdue, and put this giant into solitary confinement. Mohamet even laughed occasionally and had not been in solitary for over a year. The officers were grateful, and some said it was because he would miss his cellmate.

Chapter 8

Outside

*"Boast not thyself of tomorrow; for thou knowest
not what a day may bring forth."* Proverbs, XXVII.I

A year had passed and inmate 204 had twenty five more to serve. This did not cause him any anxiety, for he had not desire, or expectation, to ever return to the outside world he had known. He had studied how inmates become institutionalized after many years of confinement and do not wish to be free, but he was amazed at how rapidly this had happened to him. However, one never knows what the future holds and neither did inmate 204.

He was cleaning the Warden's office when the Warden arrived that day. Warden White was aware of his presence, but did not acknowledge it. The Warden quickly dug into papers and files that were waiting, and made several calls to his secretary as well as trips to file cabinets. Inmate 204 was surprised to hear the Warden speak to him.

"Strickland."

Wadus was further aware this was the first time any prison official, or officer, had referred to him by name and he quickly replied, "Yes."

"How long you been here now?"

"Just over a year sir."

"I've looked over your record a number of times and it seems you've adjusted quite well. Your health and appearance seem to have improved also."

"Yes sir."

The Warden was silent for several minutes and if as an after thought asked, "Strickland, do you know a N.C. State Senator by the name of Jacobs?"

"Sir, I have read about him in the papers but I do not know him personally."

"What do you know about him?"

"Well, I think he is from Wake County, he chairs several important committees, sits on several others, and is a top fund raiser and leader of his party. Some think he may eventually become the Governor."

Wadus knew the rule of never questioning an officer or any other prison official, let alone the Warden, but could not restrain his curiosity and asked, "Warden, may I know why you asked if I knew Senator Jacobs?"

Without thinking, or looking up from his papers, the Warden said, "Well, it's just that he seems to know—." He stopped his statement abruptly as if he were almost about to reveal too much. He concluded this rare chat by saying, "It's not important, go on with your cleaning."

Wadus finished cleaning the Warden's office, as he did each morning, but this day was not typical. He did not know the true facts, however he now knew definitely there was a skunk in the woodpile of his incarceration.

Several weeks later as he was repeating this same chore in the Warden's office the Warden received a call that was to dramatically alter the life of inmate 204 forever more. The Warden took the call and as usual inmate 204 could hear his every word but carried on as if he were deaf.

"Hello, Warden White here."

"Good morning, Warden. We have never met, my name is Trina Clark and I am the supervisor of the Governor's Mansion. I have a serious fiscal problem that has resulted in a staff shortage. I thought you might possibly come to my rescue, and I would be eternally grateful."

"I see, what did you have in mind Ms. Clark?"

"Warden, don't you have certain inmates who qualify and are assigned work details outside of Central each day?"

"Yes, we have some who meet the requirements and work outside each day."

"I desperately need a man here, mostly for outside chores, but my budget can't afford one. Could you please, please, solve my problem?"

The Warden listened carefully to this request and looked at inmate 204. He smiled and answered Ms. Clark. "Well, I might just be able to do that, in fact I have one in mind, and I'm looking at him right now." Wadus immediately knew the Warden was referring to him and worried about what he did not know.

"Well, that was quick. Is he one we can feel safe with having around the mansion?"

"Yes, I am quite sure he is, and if you would like to come over I'll be glad to go over his record and file with you. You may even see him if you wish."

"Oh no, Warden your judgment in this matter is needed, not mine. When may we expect him, soon I hope."

"He'll be there tomorrow morning around eight. Please have someone waiting who can show him what he is to do and explain what you expect. He knows our rules, and if there is any problem call Central and he will be collected immediately."

"Thank you so very much Warden. Good bye."

The Warden called inmate 204 to his desk and said, "Tomorrow morning, as soon as you eat breakfast report to the main gate. You have been assigned to an outside work detail."

The Warden thought this new assignment would please inmate 204 and was surprised when Wadus asked, "Sir, may I please be allowed to stay inside? Please give this to someone else!"

Warden White leaned back into the big chair, looked at Wadus with a frown and replied, "No, you are working on the outside starting tomorrow. Understand?"

"Yes sir."

"Well, you had best understand this also. If you intentionally do something to screw this up, things here will be real bad for you for a long time. I've told the people you are O.K. and can handle the job. Don't bring problems back on me! Do you understand 204?"

"Yes sir."

He finished the office cleaning and left. He did not know where he was being sent, or why, nor what he would be doing. There was no class in cell 101 that night. Both inmates pondered and speculated for several hours upon this sudden and atypical turn of events.

In an attempt to console Wadus, Mohamet finally said; "Well, at least they'll bring you back every evening. Besides, you'll be able to look at some them pretty ladies on the streets when you're riding in that van."

"I wish it were you doing the going and doing the looking."

"Yeah, who would look after your ass in here if I was out there all day? No, it's better you goin." Wadus could not refute this logic.

After a hurried breakfast the following morning Wadus rushed to the main entrance of Central. Seven other inmates were already there and waiting. They took a keen visual interest in their new passenger. Wadus entered the van and as it pulled away from Central he wondered what his task would be, where it would be, and why he had been assigned to an outside work detail after serving only one year? The van delivered its cargo to various state buildings until Wadus was the only remaining passenger. He knew a little about the streets of Raleigh and was aware of his approximate location but was still ignorant of his destination. Finally the van entered a gate and started up a long driveway. Wadus had a strange feeling in his stomach and could not believe he was approaching the Mansion of the Governor of the State of North Carolina! What splendid, and cruel, irony. He had been taken from the bottom of the geographic pit of North Carolina to its pinnacle within less than half an hour.

The prison van stopped where an elderly black man stood waiting and the driver said, "O.K., this is it. You be here at five sharp and don't make me wait, you got that?"

Wadus nodded and disembarked to face the man waiting for him. The man appeared to be in his late fifties and spoke in a clear and pleasantly low tone, "Hey, I'm Jefferson Carver, and they told me to meet you and to show you around. You will be helping me look after the outside of this big place. What's your name?"

Wadus pointed to the number on his prison shirt and replied, "I'm inmate 204 from Central Prison."

"Is that what you want me to call you?"

"May as well, everyone else calls me that. We are just numbers at Central."

"O.K. man, you'll be just 204."

The indoctrination tour began. Jefferson led and talked. Wadus followed and listened. Wadus recognized much of the outside for he had once toured the mansion grounds but said nothing of this to Jefferson.

As they approached a large door at the rear of the mansion Jefferson instructed, "Now in here's where they feed us our lunch about noon everyday. Be sure to clean off your shoes, and brush off your clothes, before you go in there because there's ah old black woman in there that'll give you hell! She'd da boss of th kitchen, and don't mind bossing one bit. Me, I been here so long I jes ignores her but you best listen ta what she says. The other gals in da kitchen are pretty easy ta get along with." Wadus was glad for this insight.

As he followed Jefferson into the large kitchen Wadus removed his cap and was enjoying the delicious aromas of ham, bacon, biscuits, fruit, and other sundry foods. Jefferson began to introduce him to the kitchen staff.

"This is Mrs. Clara, the lady in charge." She acknowledged Wadus with a stern and curious look. "This is Mrs. Daisy." She was the only white woman in the kitchen and looked at him and said, "Hi." "This is Amanda," who looked up and said, "Hey man, you gonna be helpin us?" Jefferson answered, "No he ain't, he's gonna be helpin me outside. This pretty young thing is Shawna." She turned with a shag like dance move to her radio music and cheerfully smiled into Wadus's face and said, "Hello, it'll be nice to have another man around."

Mrs. Clara spoke, "It would be nice if yo git yo young butt doin more dis cookin! Now I'm tellin you gal."

Shawna smiled and shagged back to her chores. Wadus observed all in silent appreciation. Taking careful visual inventory of Shawna he thought, "What grand work God is capable of." She was Afro-American with an obvious inclusion of Caucasian genes. She stood about five feet eight, her skin was very light and beautiful, her hair was long and fine, her nose and lips were thin and the corps of engineers could not have built such a beautiful body. Wadus was indeed impressed with the appearance of this young girl.

"Ya'll this is 204 from Central and Ms. Trina says he's gonna help me. If we's gets caught up I might allow him ta hep you some in here with puttin up some of dem heavy boxes in dat store room." He looked purposely at the elderly black boss lady who grunted in disgust at this announcement of authority over this new help. Wadus listened to the shag tunes on Shawna's radio. They were the same ones he had so often enjoyed dancing to in North Myrtle Beach and he glanced at the graceful moves of Shawna as Jefferson led him outside once again.

Once outside, and as if talking to himself, Jefferson said, "Lawd, Lawd, daat Shawn is some piece of work! I shore wish I had my youth!" Wadus agreed with his appraisal of the young girl but did not share his desire to regain spent years.

Jefferson showed inmate 204 the building where all of the maintenance equipment was stored. There were several riding lawn mowers, different power tools, vacuum cleaners, paints, and many types of brooms and cleaning materials. Wadus was much relieved by now, for at least he knew where he would be and what he would be doing. The WHY of it all was still a mystery and troubled him.

The morning was spent following, and listening, to Jefferson's instructions, and Wadus came to believe his boss was a good man. As both men ate their lunch at a small kitchen table Wadus was hard put to decide what he enjoyed the most. Was it the wonderful taste of the food, or Shawna's rhythmic moves to the oldies and goldies tunes of the fifties and sixties, or was it the memories of the coast which were conjured up in his mind? Regardless, he thoroughly and silently enjoyed it all.

Wadus spent that first afternoon doing many small chores that Jefferson assigned. The prison van arrived promptly at five and Wadus was waiting. He was the first inmate collected and wondered why. Eventually the others were picked up and all were delivered back to Central.

As Wadus approached the table where Mohamet ate his evening meal it was obvious his cellmate had spent an anxious day and was glad to see him. Once in cell 101 and locked down for the night Wadus began answering questions and telling Mohamet of the events of the day. Both men were still perplexed and asked each other questions of how, and why, which neither had answers to. After repeating, rethinking, and re-discussing everything for several hours each of them sat silent for a long time.

Mohamet finally said, "Man, I tell you what I think. You better be more careful around that house than you have to be in here."

"Why is that Mohamet?" He had learned to respect this man's innate ability to sense danger when none was apparent.

"I'll tell you why. Cause you gonna be around ah bunch of rich people. I don't trust them. Give'em the chance and they'll do you worse than that white trash would have done you that day in the bathroom. Watch'em!"

Wadus understood his meaning and after briefly thinking said, "Well, I won't be around those people, I'll be outside doing yard work and other chores."

"Just remember what Kabul's tellin ya, watch your own ass!"

Wadus pondered the truth to what he had heard but did not answer. He was exhausted from the tension and chores of the day and as he drifted into sleep he could see Shawna's sensuous movements and hear the beach music he loved.

Chapter 9

The Comfort Zone
"This world's a bubble." Bacon

The Governor of North Carolina was Thomas C. Trout. He had been elected in 1988 at the age of forty-eight. His wife's name was Grace, she was forty-six, and they had a daughter, Debra who was sixteen.

Thomas Trout had been reared in the mountains of Wilkes County. He was from a hard working middle-class family who had placed a great priority upon education. They had greatly sacrificed so their son could attend the University of North Carolina and go on to receive his law degree from the same university. He had practiced law in Wilkesboro, N.C. and had been extremely successful. He married at age thirty, and his wife had given birth to their only child two years later. He had become well known in northwestern North Carolina and was finally induced into politics when he was in his early forties. He was a Democrat and eventually elected Governor.

Wadus Strickland's only knowledge of this man and his family was from what he had learned through the news media. The Governor's first year in office had been politically routine and without any major legislation or controversy. Nevertheless, the eternal sea of politics is dark and deep. The bill collectors would eventually demand payment and the tab would be higher than this good man expected or was willing to pay.

Five days each week for the next eight months inmate 204 went to the number one residency in North Carolina. Mohamet had been somewhat correct and Wadus came to look forward to the ride to and from the mansion each day. He enjoyed the scenes and observing the people and activity on the busy Raleigh streets. Never, however, did he wish to be part of it and was always glad to return to Central Prison each evening and the sanctuary of cell 101.

His work was not physically difficult and absolutely void of mental responsibilities. Jefferson assigned chores each day. Wadus went from one to the next, no brain, no pain. He quite often saw the Governor, his wife, or the child, arriving at or leaving the mansion. There had been no close contact between him and the residents of this mansion and to them he was only another carbon unit unseen and non-existent. Wadus liked this and made every attempt to perpetuate this relationship. After these many months he was very familiar with the grounds and the outside of the mansion. Other than the kitchen he knew very little of the inside of the structure.

Each day he and Jefferson had their noon meal in the kitchen. This was the high point of each day for Wadus, and he looked forward to this short time more and more. The meals were always excellent as they ate the same food that was prepared for the Governor and his family. Yes, the food was good, but the best part of the meal was just being in the same area with the female cooks. Wadus rarely spoke, only if spoken to, but heard every word and observed every movement. Shawna's radio constantly played the old and new beach shag tunes. It amused Wadus to watch the war of decibels between Shawna and Mrs. Clara the boss lady. Up then down, followed by comments from the master, up and down, depending upon which one was nearer to the radio. Shawna was constantly fussed at by the elderly black lady, but it was obvious she could not hide her affection for this beautiful and high-spirited young girl. Shawna was usually the one who would prepare his and Jefferson's plates and dancingly deliver them while she hummed, sang, and kidded Jefferson. One day as the two meals were placed upon the table she looked directly into Wadus's eyes and demanded, "Man, what's your name? I been wanting to know that a long time, and besides when I want to talk to a man I don't want to use no number! Come on now, what's your name?"

Wadus felt compelled to answer and said, "Wadus."

"Wadus. Ya'll hear that, this is Wadus. Now what's the last name?"

"Strickland."

"I've never heard the name Wadus before but I have Strickland. Are you Indian?"

Wadus was not accustomed to such an inquiry but observed the others were quite interested in his responses so he slowly said, "Well, I was born, and reared, in Robeson County so there's a good chance that part of me is Lumbee Indian."

"Yeah, I've heard a lot about them. They talk real funny like don't they?"

"Yes, many of them still use an Elizabethan dialect and accent."

"Really, tell me what that means. I want to know all about the Lumbee Indians."

"Chil leave da man be so's he can eat his food. He's got ta get back ta work."

Wadus was relieved as he felt somewhat tense. It had been a very long time since he had enjoyed a conversation with a female and besides, Jefferson was right, work waited outside.

Wadus came to consider the kitchen his "comfort zone." He had to pass through it several times each day in order to use a bathroom which joined one of the rooms used to store food supplies. He eventually asked Mrs. Clara if he could put away some boxes of canned goods for her. It would give him a little more time in this comfort zone.

The boss lady snapped, "Snowball, ain't dat old black fool out dey got nough work fo you? He'll be in here argin at me, dee old fool. Go head Snowball, puts dem boxes in dat storeroom." Wadus did as he was told wondering how she had decided on the name of "Snowball" for him. As he left the kitchen Mrs. Clara said, "Thank ya, Snowball." Once outside Wadus stopped for a moment, shook his head, and laughed for the first time in over a year.

As time passed Wadus was more and more a common sight in the kitchen when he had any spare time. He was no longer 204. He was either "Snowball" to Mrs. Clara or "Wadus" to the others. It was obvious they enjoyed his company as much as he enjoyed being present. There were endless observations, discussions, and questions. They all seemed to rely upon him to answer, confirm, refute, almost every issue. No matter how hard he tried they would not allow him to hide in the background and his charisma increased. Quite often now Mrs. Clara would hand him some delicious morsel all wrapped-up and say, "Snowball, you takes dis home with you and eat it later on."

Wadus would always give these treats to Mohamet who enjoyed them but appeared to value having been remembered by his cellmate more. Most nights now were spent relating the events of the day to Mohamet and less and less time on studies. Wadus was, more and more, impressed by the intellectual leap his cellmate and close friend had made.

Wadus did try desperately to remain silent, withdrawn, and unfeeling, but it seemed to only add to his mystique. Many times he would only answer a question with a question, shake his head, or say, "What do you think?" He knew much more about his daytime companions than they knew about him and he wanted to keep it that way. At times, however, he would forget and be sucked-in to revelations which he had rather have kept to himself. It was especially difficult when confronted by the vivacious Shawna. One such day he was putting away supplies, and as he passed Shawna she extended her arm and hand as she did some very good shag movements. Without thinking Wadus took her hand, stood and without moving his feet, turned her hand as if shagging with her, pulled her by him, swung her arm over her head and reversed the same movement. He never moved his frame, only his hand and arm. Mrs. Clara watched, seemed amused, but said nothing. Shawna did not intend to be so demure. Backing up and placing her hands on her hips and with surprise all over her pretty face exclaimed, "Wadus, you got some bad moves. Do you know how to shag?"

"Some."

"I've got a feeling it's more than just some. Where did you learn to shag?"

Wadus smiled for it seemed she thought he had been in prison all of his life and opened-up, "Shawna, the shag started in the fifties and most of the music you listen to on your radio, and shag to, came out of the fifties and sixties. It's become more popular today than ever. In fact it has been declared the official state dance of South Carolina."

"Where did you shag?"

"All over. We had dances and as a matter of fact Channel 13 in Florence, S.C. had a Saturday morning shag hour. They called it "Party Time." Each Saturday a group of boys and girls from a certain school would be invited to dance on that show from eleven until twelve. The judges selected a winning couple and they were invited back the following week to compete against students from a different school. My partner and I won twice and were first runner ups the third week."

Shawna reacted as though Wadus had now become a real human being. A bond was formed. Age, race, appearance, inmate, none was important to this young woman for now they were peers.

"Alright man, you wicked bad. We gonna have to shag some."

Mrs. Clara snapped, "Not in dis kitchen you ain't! Sides, how's Snowball gonna do any shaggin him locked-up in dat jailhouse. You foolish gal."

Shawna refused to relent and asked, "When was the last time you went shagging and where?"

"Well, I have a home on the coast near North Myrtle Beach and used to hang-out and shag a lot at Fat Harold's Beach Club, the Spanish Galleon, Ducks, Poo's, and a number of other places. I was there a lot before going to prison."

"Cool man! Wadus, when do you get out? I want to shag with you at the beach."

This statement slapped Wadus back into the real world. He looked silently at Shawna, shook his head, picked-up another box and vanished into the storeroom. He remained in there for a short time and thought, "why, why, why did I do that? Why did I let her inside my head for even that much? It won't happen again. Twenty-five years to serve and I'm talking about shagging. I am a fool!"

Chapter 10

Dreaming Dreams

*"Passion is universal humanity. Without
it religion, history, romance and art
would be useless."* Balzac

Wadus continued his monotonous daily routine of chores
and attempted not to come in contact with any other
mansion occupants, or staff, other than Jefferson and
his friends in the kitchen. He remembered the Indian
philosopher's answer to Alexander the Great's question, "What
is the most cunning beast on earth?" The philosopher had
answered, "That beast which man has not yet discovered."
Wadus did not wish to be discovered by any additional
persons. Indeed, he felt a sense of security in his obscurity, for
who bothers with a thing they do not know exists? He thought
of the Governor, rich persons, famous actors, athletes, and
entertainers who are constantly hounded by the media. Yes,
they were prisoners also and would probably pay much for a
few precious hours, or days, they could move about in
obscurity as millions of common Americans do each day! But
they could not for mammon had purchased their freedom,
privacy, and peace. He did not envy such persons. Yet, even
the whip-poor-will is sometimes sighted and disturbed. The
routine of inmate 204 was about to be disturbed!

As Jefferson and Wadus ate their lunches that day Ms.
Clark, the mansion supervisor, entered the kitchen. Wadus was
alert and keenly observed her as she approached them with a

rapid take-charge gait. She was a very attractive woman, about five feet eight inches tall, around 120 pounds, emerald eyes, a pleasant voice, and a beautifully shaped figure. Wadus stood as she arrived in front of them. She looked down at Jefferson and said, "Jefferson, I am very sorry, however, I must take your outside helper away from you for awhile. One of the house keepers is ill, and I am not sure when, if ever, she will return." Wadus began to experience that terrible sensation in his stomach as he realized he was about to lose his security by obscurity and would be pushed into different human traffic. Jefferson looked, and listened, but did not express any objections at the prospect of losing the labor of inmate 204.

Ms. Clark looked at Wadus and asked, "What is your name?"

Wadus silently pointed to the number 204 on his faded blue prison shirt.

Ms. Clark observed it and said, "O.K. fine. Starting this afternoon you will be doing house cleaning chores, up and downstairs, helping in here, and any other chore you are needed for. Do you understand?"

"Yes ma'am."

"Mrs. Clara will you show him where everything is and get him started right after he finishes lunch?" Mrs. Clara indicated she would and Ms. Clark quickly left the kitchen.

Shawna snapped, "I'd like to show her where to get started."

"Huss now gal, don't let yo big mouth get yo little butt in trouble."

"I don't care Mrs. Clara, I don't like that tight-ass white woman." She glanced at Wadus and with a beautiful smile said, "I know what she needs, right Wadus."

"Gal I done tol ya ta hush now! Come on Snowball, I show ya where ever thang is an where ta git started." She led him to a utility room and introduced him to all the necessary tools for his new duties. She handed him a large can of furniture polish, towels, and escorted him to the inside entrance of the mansion. There were huge hardwood doors and much elaborate woodwork. He was told where to find a ladder to reach the high areas and cautioned not to scratch the beautiful hardwood floors.

Wadus was no virgin in this type of work for he had done all of his own cleaning and house work for a number of years and had cleaned most of Central Prison many times. The area here to be cleaned was only far more elegant.

Wadus had been polishing for several hours working his way from the entrance. He had seen Ms. Clark pass by several times but ignored her presence as she ignored his. Just after four in the afternoon the large front door opened and a young girl entered carrying a big bag of books over her right shoulder. It was Debra Trout, the Governor's daughter. She was sixteen, blond, blue eyes, about five feet six inches tall, and physically well developed for her years. She had almost started to make her way up the long stairway when she realized there was a different person in her domestic world. She stopped, walked over to Wadus and asked, "Who are you?"

Wadus said nothing and silently pointed, once again, to the number on his prison shirt.

The young girl gazed at it for a moment and looked him in the face and exclaimed, "My God are you a convict?"

"Yes ma'am, from Central Prison."

"What are you doing in here?"

Wadus thought this to be a dumb question and slightly lifted the polish and towel he held.

"How long are you going to be here?"

"I don't know how long I'll be working inside but I have been working outside for a number of months." Sensing her anxiety he added, "I go back to Central everyday at five o'clock."

"Well, just stay away from me!"

"Yes ma'am."

The young girl made her way upstairs rapidly and once out of sight began calling, "Mom, Mom, Mom, where are you?"

Wadus hoped her evident objections to his presence would outweigh Ms. Clark's authority and that he would soon be with Jefferson again. This was not to be!

Several days later Debra brought one of her girl friends home with her after school. Wadus had tried to make sure his cleaning duties at that time of day were well out of her usual route, however, she was not to be avoided on this day. He could hear the sound of their voices but not what was being said. Both girls began searching, room by room, calling, "204, 204, 204, where are you?" followed by silly teen giggles. Suddenly they appeared in the large den where Wadus cleaned. "204, didn't you hear me calling you?"

"I thought I heard something but wasn't sure what."

"Well, answer when you think someone might be calling you. Kelly, this is our cleaning man, he's a convict. They take him back to Central every night and bring him back the next day." Wadus was humiliated and felt ashamed but had no animosity toward these youngsters. He knew after almost thirty years as a teacher and understood their over-active hormones and absence of cerebral maturation that is typical at their age.

They walked over very close to him and Debra pointed to his shirt, "See, his number is 204."

"Wow, like man, that's so cool. Hey, can you get me one of those shirts?"

Wadus was more than a little shocked and replied, "No ma'am, I can't."

The young girls exchanged comments concerning this captive house cleaner, giggled some more and then were interrupted by Mrs. Trout's call from down the hallway, "Debra, Debra." The girls quickly disappeared to answer the call.

Wadus made all possible effort to do his upstairs cleaning chores when he was relatively sure Mr. Trout and Debra were not in the mansion. He was able to accomplish this most of the time. He did, however, begin to be aware that Ms. Clark appeared more and more often where ever he happened to be cleaning and would ask trivial questions. He speculated upon her possible motives.

When Wadus arrived each morning he lingered as long as possible in the kitchen before venturing into other parts of the mansion. He hoped to avoid the occupants and his strategy worked most of the time. The Governor was usually out of the mansion by nine and often sooner if he had to be away from Raleigh. Mrs. Trout seemed to have even more duties, obligations, and commitments than the Governor. There were always a couple of Highway Troopers and a couple of plain clothes BCI officers on the premises. Many mornings the Governor ate his breakfast alone in the large dinning room.

Wadus had been performing his new cleaning duties for a number of weeks before coming face to face with Thomas C. Trout, the Governor of North Carolina. As the Governor had his breakfast on this particular morning he called for more coffee. All in the kitchen were extremely busy because Mrs. Daisy had not come in due to illness. Mrs. Clara quickly ordered, "Snowball, git dat coffee pot and take da Governor some coffee." Wadus had no choice and obeyed. Taking the coffee he entered the room and walked to where the Governor sat eating and reading the News and Observer newspaper. As Wadus filled the cup the Governor glanced upward and stared at him.

"You must be the man from Central who has been helping out around the mansion."

"Yes sir," and as he pointed to the number on his shirt asked, "would you like anything else sir?"

"No". Wadus turned to retreat from the room but was stopped as the Governor said, "Wait a moment, I'd like to speak with you." Wadus did as instructed and the Governor continued, "How long have you been here and how is it our paths have never crossed until now?"

"I have been helping Jefferson for a number of months but several weeks ago Ms. Clark changed my duties to cleaning on the inside."

"I see. I also see your number, what is your name?"

"Wadus Strickland sir."

"How much time did you get?"

"Twenty six years sir."

"Twenty six, how old are you?"

"I recently became fifty sir."

The Governor hesitated as if wondering if this man had the longevity to ever know freedom again. He said, "Well Wadus, my daughter expressed some apprehension about your presence inside of the house. I called Warden White, and he assured me there was no need to be concerned. Was he correct?"

"Yes sir. I try to do my cleaning so I will stay out of your wife and daughter's sight."

"That isn't necessary as long as you're not a threat and don't try to leave."

"Sir, I am no threat to anyone and have no intention of trying to escape."

"That's good to know. That'll be all."

The Governor was pressing a button on the inter-com system as Wadus left the room. Soon Ms. Clark was standing before him.

"Yes sir, did you want to see me?"

"Yes, Ms. Clark I just spoke with the inmate who is helping with the inside house keeping. How is he working out?"

"Just great sir. He does a good job, is very polite, very quiet, and I've noticed he is very careful in trying not to disturb anyone. I understand he is extremely well educated."

The Governor smiled as he had seldom detected such enthusiasm from this woman and said, "I am glad you are so pleased with him Ms. Clark. Now, get him a few of those white waist jackets to wear over that prison shirt. It will look much better, especially if my wife or daughter should have guests over. It may even help them forget he's an inmate from Central Prison."

"Yes sir, I'll do that this morning." The Governor rose and exited the room and mansion for his duties.

Wadus was summoned to Ms. Clark's office just before three that afternoon. Entering he said, "Yes ma'am, you wanted to see me?"

"Yes, I have something for you." She walked to a box and pulled out one of the white waistcoats and held it to his chest and shoulders. "I think I have guessed your correct size. Put this on over your shirt. The Governor requested that you wear one of these around the mansion and I think it is a splendid idea." Wadus put the jacket on and buttoned it up as Ms. Clark watched. The jacket had long sleeves and a banded collar. Ms. Clark circled him for further inspection and said, "That looks very nice. Take this box, you have five jackets, one for each day, O.K.?"

"Yes ma'am." He collected the box of jackets and left her office and went to the kitchen. As he entered he was immediately noticed by Shawna who did a quick double-take and in her exuberant dancing disposition exclaimed, "Hey Wadus, look at you man. You getting down bad honey."

71

Coming over she turned him around slowly for further appraisal. "Wadus, my main man, lookin good honey." Shawna smiled, danced, and the other ladies commented and nodded their approval.

Wadus left the kitchen and went to the storeroom where he would leave his "gift." He lingered for some time, just looking at the box. He felt very strange. He had actually received a "gift." He was inmate 204, a fifty-year-old convict, a man with no desire to look backward and only one reason to look forward. He was unaccustomed to being the recipient of anything nice. He thought of how his life had been devoured by years of working, giving, and providing "things" which he thought others needed or wanted. He had always been good at giving but very awkward when receiving. Yet he felt pleased at having received this N.C. State gift. Yes he would indeed be glad to wear these jackets and agreed with the Governor's logic and decision.

He wore his white jackets daily and in the coming weeks guests thought he was just another mansion employee and never imagined him to be an inmate. He became more and more proficient in his chores and also organizing them as to avoid the primary residents. He saw Ms. Clark more and more and it became more and more difficult to evade her observations of whatever he was doing. He felt as though she distrusted him less, rather than more, with each passing day and wanted to find some justification for such apprehensions. Maybe he would soon be back with his friend at Central. That would be O.K.; he could deal with it.

Late one afternoon she approached him and asked very politely, "Wadus, will you clean my office first thing tomorrow morning? It's an awful mess." This seemed out of character, and he noted it was the first time she had ever called him "Wadus." He didn't realize she knew his name.

"Yes ma'am, I'll be glad to."

The following morning he hastened to do as she had requested. Ms. Clark entered her office sooner than he had expected, and upon doing so Wadus was quickly aware she had closed the door behind her.

She turned and cheerfully said, "Good morning Wadus."

Looking at her in surprise Wadus replied, "Good— morning ma'am." His shock and hesitation was quite obvious as he stood and beheld the new person whom he had seen as an entirely different female the previous day. Her hair, usually worn in a twisted bundle on top of her head, now flowed long down her back and shoulders releasing its radiant dark redness. The glasses were absent. She wore high heels and a tasteful gray dress perfectly tailored to balance conservatism and yet enhance her beautifully formed body. Wadus had always admired beauty in all of nature's creation and silently thought she was possibly one of the most beautiful ladies he had ever seen. He further thought of how often such beauty is so close by, and how often we fail to see it.

Wadus, although somewhat reluctant to do so, ventured to be bold and said, "Ms. Clark, I hope you won't think I'm being forward but you look absolutely superb today. Different but beautifully different."

This appeared to make all of her obvious efforts worthwhile and she said, "Why thank you Wadus. I didn't think anyone would notice. You really think so?"

"Oh yes ma'am, I sincerely know so, and I'm sure I will not be alone in my thinking."

This gorgeous creature smiled with feminine satisfaction as she sat down behind her desk. Wadus continued his polishing but could not ignore the delicious fragrance that now filled the room. It had been several years, and he could not be certain, yet he was relatively confident her perfume was Chanel #5. He wanted to just close his eyes and drift backward in time as the scent invaded his nostrils stimulating neurological flashes and scenes much as lightening does on a dark night.

"Darn this old desk, this drawer gets stuck and is so difficult sometimes. Wadus will you help me please?"

"Yes ma'am." He left the polishing and went to the desk drawer next to where Ms. Clark sat.

As he bent down she turned slightly, leaned over and said, "Now if I can just get accustomed to these contact lens."

Wadus glanced up into her gorgeous and somewhat wet eyes and said, "Oh you will, and it'll will be worth all the discomfort." As he attempted to open the drawer her hair dropped onto his left arm and she leaned over closer to him and the drawer. Half-turned she leaned closer and closer. Her long hair tickled his left hand, and he could not ignore her sensual and beautifully formed legs that were now pressing against his leg. Suddenly she reached down as if to help pull the drawer open but placed her hand upon the back of his. She gently, but firmly, squeezed his left hand. Wadus looked up quickly and stared into an equal stare. He felt as though he were viewing glittering stars on a cool, clear, Carolina night. He tried to stand but his legs failed him much the same way they had done for a different reason his first night in cell 101.

Still squeezing his hand she softly asked, "Wadus, how old are you?"

"I—I—I'm fifty."

"I just became thirty four recently."

"That's a wonderful age Ms. Clark."

"Well, I don't feel so wonderful."

"Why not, what's wrong?"

Trina Clark replied without reservation, but inmate 204 was not prepared for the words he was about to hear. She said, "You are what's wrong Wadus. That day I walked into the kitchen and you stood up and looked directly into my face pimples ran all over my body. It seemed I was surrounded by something and it was pulling me across the room toward you. I've never experienced anything like that sensation, it was ghostly, but enchanting. It actually felt as though my entire body was being penetrated and taken over. Wadus, who are you? What are you? You are so silent, yet speak very loudly. Your presence, even as an inmate, commands and demands attention. What is it that envelopes you and gives you an unasked for status? Why do I have this weird feeling that you are the most unique person I have ever known, or will know? Why do I have erotic thoughts, and dreams, of being with you? Why do I feel so completely at ease, and good inside, confessing these intimate desires to you? Why do I want to make love to you more than anything I have ever desired in my entire life?"

Wadus did not move for several moments and she put her hand upon his head and slowly raked her long slender fingers down through his long silver hair. He forced himself to rise slowly to his feet. He turned and looked down into complete and unspoiled beauty and desire. She sat but extended her arms and hands upward to him. He gently took her hands and lifted her from the chair. Putting both arms around him tightly she whispered, "Wadus, lock the door." He did not move but put his arms around her and silently thought this might be the last moment of honest, good, and pure passion he would ever experience. She repeated, "Lock the door Wadus, please."

He gazed into her beautiful eyes, slightly moved his head side to side, and softly said, "No Trina darling, you cannot come into my world! I do not live, I only breathe, in a world where depression is king. Ugliness is art. Hope has died. Optimism is extinct, and if God cancelled tomorrow there would be more joy than sorrow. You are too precious. What you are is too rare and beautiful to be given to me. You are too pure and sensual; none of these exist in my world. No, I cannot, I will not, take you into that world. If God, and the State, would allow it, I would take you to my little kingdom by the sea and make you the axis of my life. I would make love to you, cherish you, protect you, and you would come to understand why you have the feelings you now cannot understand. Please, let me come into your world if only for a moment. Please, just let me hold you, smell you, and dream dreams of what life would be like with you in my little kingdom."

Wadus moved his hands firmly, sensually, down her back and onto her buttocks as he pulled her close to his body. His penis swelled and throbbed against her soft stomach. She breathed rapidly and drew him even tighter. She slid her hand between their bodies and taking his manhood she squeezed and worked it, repeating, "Wadus, Wadus, oh Wadus, I love you." They kissed long and passionately.

He could endure it no longer. Against all his male instincts, and desires, he gently pushed her away. He said, "Oh Trina, I cannot survive in my world if I allow myself to want. Thank you for the most beautiful experience of my life. Thank you, darling. Only you and I must never share these precious moments, but know you will always be in my mind and a big part of my soul."

Wadus gathered his cleaning materials and exited Ms. Clark's office. She remained there for sometime. He, nor she, would ever reveal to anyone what had transpired behind that closed door. Neither, however, would ever be the same again.

That night, and many future nights in the years to come, they would both relive the events of that very special day, and both would dream dreams of their love in a small kingdom by the sea.

Chapter II

Caught Off Guard

*"Treachery, though at first very cautious,
in the end betrays itself."* Livy

The following morning Wadus had already begun dusting and polishing near the main entrance when the Governor passed on his way out. He was momentarily detained by Ms. Clark's call, "Governor, may I have just a moment before you leave?"

"Yes," as he turned to face the radically different appearance of the mansion supervisor. Wadus smiled as he observed the shocked Governor's rapid up, and down, viewing of Ms. Clark.

"Ms. Clark? You are Ms. Clark?"

"Of course I am."

"What in the world have you done? You look like an entirely different person."

"You don't approve sir?"

"I not only approve, I applaud you. You are an extremely more attractive lady. Who's the lucky man who inspired such a change?"

"That sir I cannot reveal."

"And why not?"

"I don't want to share any of him with anyone. Now, about the cocktail party on Thursday evening." After finishing her inquiry of the Governor Ms. Clark turned, and as she passed looked at Wadus with a pleasant smile and gave him a quick wink.

In the months, and years to come, there would be little physical contact between Wadus Strickland and Ms. Clark. There were, however, hundreds of hours of verbal communication. She was drawn closer, and closer, until it seemed to her their souls had mated in passionate love. She longed for the physical and prayed that someday it might be possible. Until then she knew she would always be held a willing prisoner by inmate 204. She was fascinated by his stories. His young years in Robeson County, his love for his home on the coast, and thought of herself as an extension of this man. She wanted him as her own and wanted to be owned by him. Wadus was unable to let even her share the memories of his Jamie. He could not possibly expect her to understand what he truly longed for, to be with his son!

Mohamet's advice, and warning, had been sound. Wadus was compelled to recall it late one afternoon as he cleaned one of the upstairs bathrooms.

It was almost time to put things away and hurry to meet the prison van. Wadus worked rapidly cleaning the mirror and countertops in this large and elaborate bathroom. He thought only of finishing and of the fact he was behind his normal schedule.

Suddenly Debra Trout stepped into the bathroom and closed the door behind her. Wadus was shocked and even more terrified than when attacked by the four men at Central. Holding glass cleaner in one hand and towel in the other he faced the young girl and said, "Now, wait just a minute young lady!"

She reached over quickly, and forcefully, swept everything in arms reach from the counter top. She then stood back against the door, looked at him, and smiled. Suddenly she ripped open her blouse with both hands tearing the material and sending buttons scattering to the floor. She then snatched opened the door and ran down the hallway screaming loudly and hysterically. Running down the stairs she shouted, "HELP! HELP! HELP! THAT PRISONER ATTACKED ME!" She was met and embraced at the bottom of the stairs by Mrs. Trout who also began screaming and calling for help.

Still holding the cleaning materials Wadus leaned back against the counter and lowered his head as he waited for what he knew would be upon him very soon. A number of thoughts raced through his mind but none were of the child's treachery. His first thought was of Ms. Clark and of his friends in the kitchen. His thoughts of their thoughts, and opinions, of him slashed at his heart with the fury of the Grim Reaper's blade. How hurt Ms. Clark would be, and how she would be blamed for his presence in the house. How she would weep, and how he wished he could hold her and kiss away her tears. He prayed she would know the truth in her heart!

He could hear the heavy, fast, and pounding footsteps coming up the stairs. A security officer and highway trooper ran into the bathroom. With speed, and force, they grabbed and threw him out of the bathroom into the wall across the hall. One pinned him against the wall as the other rapidly handcuffed his arms behind him. Wadus said nothing. The glass cleaner and towel fell to the floor. They hastily dragged him down the stairs. By the time they reached the bottom of the stairs there was total pandemonium. Mrs. Trout embraced her screaming child, there were loud voices as people rushed from other parts of the mansion. He looked directly into Mrs. Trout's face as he was rushed by and could hear Ms. Clark shouting, "What's wrong?" as she too came to investigate. She arrived to see Wadus being rushed through the front entrance and down the steps to a waiting patrol unit. The patrol unit was rapidly underway, and as it sped from the grounds Wadus could see his evening ride arriving.

As Ms. Clark approached Mrs. Trout and the sobbing child Mrs. Trout exclaimed harshly, "That convict you brought into this house just attacked my child!" She then began to help Debra upstairs toward her bedroom. Ms. Clark stood in silent horror and disbelief.

Having helped her daughter to her bed Mrs. Trout phoned the Governor's office. He was in conference but took the call. The Governor jumped to his feet as the events were related to him.

"I'm on my way right now. Grace, tell everyone, the complete staff, to remain there until I can speak with them!" The Governor apologized and left for the mansion

79

immediately. As he rushed through the entrance he was met by his wife. He asked, "Is Debra alright?"

"Yes, she was able to get away from that man. The doctor is on his way, she needs something to calm her down. Tom, I want that man to stay in prison for the rest of his life!"

"Grace honey, let me think please."

They both hurried to Debra's bedroom and began trying to console her. The Dr. arrived and the Governor went downstairs where the entire staff were waiting as instructed.

The Governor spoke to the entire group. "We have had a tragic, and unfortunate, incident take place here this afternoon. My daughter was very lucky. This will be with her for a very long time. I don't intend to have anyone make it anymore difficult for her. Now, you are not to repeat anything that has occurred here today to anyone, not even to members of your own families. Does everyone understand the importance of what I am saying?" They all acknowledged they understood and would comply. All except Ms. Clark were dismissed. The Governor told her she had shown poor judgment in allowing an inmate to be inside the mansion. After much reprimanding she was told to leave for the evening. The Governor went to the mansion office and phoned Warden White at Central Prison. The Warden had left for the day and was en route to his home. Thirty minutes later the Governor reached him there.

"Warden this is the Governor. That inmate you sent over here attacked my little girl this afternoon!"

"What?" He could not believe what he was hearing.

"That's right. Now, I want that inmate's file on my desk by the time I arrive in my office tomorrow morning. I want to go over it thoroughly and then we will talk again."

"Yes sir, it will be there." The conversation ended, and the Warden stood as if in a trance. He did not understand how he could have misjudged inmate 204 so incorrectly. He also thought his position as Warden might well be in jeopardy for having recommended this inmate for such duty. He then called Central and was informed the inmate had arrived and was already locked away in solitary confinement.

"Good, don't allow him any contact with anyone." But three people can keep a secret only if two are dead, and bad news travels extremely fast behind prison walls.

Wadus had been taken directly to Central and turned over to several officers who were awaiting his arrival. One of the officers who had driven him there said, "This bastard attacked the Governor's little girl!" Wadus continued to remain silent but was relatively confident of what was to come. Two officers were ordered to take him immediately to solitary. The Warden would later decide for how long. The inmate was roughly, and hurriedly, pushed along by the officer behind him. As they turned a corner and were not far from their destination, Wadus felt the officer's heavy stick come into his back with fury. He fell against the wall in great pain, and as he turned his head received another loud hard whack above the left eye. He felt the skin part and blood flow. He sank downward but was jerked up and sped along to a cell another thirty feet down the narrow hall. An officer opened the cell and he was pushed in still standing. He was then struck a number of times, once again in the face, the rest of the blows were to his mid body. He lay unconscious on the floor as the officers withdrew and locked the door.

Mohamet, as usual, sat alone at the large table as he watched the entrance for his cellmate to appear for the evening meal. The meal was finished and inmate 204 was not present. Mohamet became increasingly anxious as his instincts told him something was wrong. The other inmates made note of the absence of Mohamet's companion, and there was an unusual amount of mumbling in the large mess hall. Mohamet finished, walked to the disposal area and with obvious agitation slammed tray, dishes, and everything into one large trash container. Two officers quickly approached him. They stopped several feet away as Mohamet turned to face them. One of the officers asked, "What's your problem Kabul?" There was no reply and the officer ordered, "Just don't make trouble, move along!"

The inmate communication system was always excellent and this evening was no exception. By the time all were back in their cells and locked down, news was leaping from cell to cell. Inmate 204 had assaulted a young girl and was in solitary! Most of the inmates had no reason to doubt the truth of this news and accepted it as such. When Mohamet received this information he reverted to a primitive, and violent, personality.

He grasped the cell bars and shouted, "Lying white bastards!" He continued to shout obscenities that were heard by inmates and officers alike. His comrades endorsed his every statement and cheered him on. Several officers rushed to cell 101.

"Shut up Kabul and back away from that door!"

"Fuck you!"

The officer struck at his arm through the bars but Mohamet was quicker and avoiding the blow said, "Bring your sorry white trash ass, and your fuckin stick, in here and hit me mother-fucker. I'll see if your worthless tight ass can take it all. Come on in you white piece of shit!" By now there was an uproar from all cells and all officers knew a riot was in the embryonic stage. Whistles blew, officers took their positions, and a special squad of five especially trained to subdue violent inmates were rushed to cell 101. Mohamet was keenly aware of their every move, for it would not be his first trip to solitary. He also knew how many inmates often had terrible "accidents" during the final few feet of the journey. He did not care, he had to know his friend, tutor, and companion was alright! Solitary was a price he would gladly pay. The squad, appearing much as ninja turtles in their helmets and armor, arrived quickly in front of cell 101. Mohamet backed far into the cell as the door opened and the squad rushed in. He stood calmly and extended both arms outward with open palms up. The special squad was not expecting this and were visibly shocked, and relieved, at Mohamet's lack of resistance. They rapidly put cuffs on him and rushed toward solitary confinement. Toilet paper and dozens of different items were thrown from cells and the ground level was now covered with trash. With Mohamet's removal the situation began to de-escalate and within an hour things were back to near normal.

As the squad neared the solitary cells Mohamet warned, "Now man don't hit me with them sticks. I ain't gonna give you no trouble unless you do. I promise I ain't, but if any of you hit me I'm gonna hurt some of you real bad." The riot squad knew this was no idle threat, and none laid a stick on this man.

He was locked in a cell that was four away from where Wadus lay unconscious. As soon as the officers were gone he began to call in a very low voice, "Wadus, where are you man?" He repeated this every few minutes for the next several hours.

At first Wadus thought he was dreaming, for in the distance he could hear a low voice but in his semi-conscious condition could not understand it or react to it. Finally, he was able to snake himself to the door using the small amount of light from the narrow opening through which food was passed. He sat with his back against the door trying to clear his head and gain more mobility. He asked, "Mohamet is that you?"

Mohamet was much relieved to hear his response and said, "Yeah man it's me. You alright man?"

Wadus answered slowly, "I'm alive—but I don't know the extent of the damages yet."

"They beat yo bad Wadus? Them bastards."

"Well, I don't know what the usual ration is, but I think I was out by the time the last course was served."

"Can you stand-up man? You got any broke bones man?"

Wadus forced a painful smile and said, "No and no. I might have some fractured ribs, my right eye is closed, and there's a respectable cut over it."

"Stand-up man, stand-up. Damn your white ass, don't let the bastards beat you man!"

"Mohamet what are you doing down here?"

"Man, I come to see if you were still alive, you ain't able to take much of a beatin an live!"

"I thought you had learned to think before you act Mohamet!"

"Fuck the thinking! Man, you thinks too much! Sometimes you just got to do and not think!"

Wadus did not answer immediately as he considered the certain amount of truth and logic in Mohamet's statement.

"Look man, sometimes there' not time to think if you want to stay alive. Sometimes there's things that means more to you than to have to even think about them. Them times you just acts."

Wadus hesitated as he remembered that terrible June afternoon and submissively said, "You are right, you are right, there are those times."

Mohamet felt great at having won his point and quickly replied, "You damn straight man, I knows I'm right."

"Mohamet, I can't see in here. What's in this room?"

"Man, there's cot, a toilet, and a wash basin. Can you get to'em?"

"I'm gonna try. I've got to clean this cut over my eye."

"Them fools say you attacked a young girl. I knowed better. I told you to watch your ass around them folks."

"Thank you, Mohamet. I tried to watch for everything but I got caught off-guard, didn't have a chance to run."

"Nobody but me gonna believe you anyways so you just got to be tough. You got to be like one of them lean wolves man."

Wadus crawled away from the door to explore the dark as his friend continued to give him all the support possible. The last he could hear was Mohamet's question, "Hey Wadus, man which way is east from where we is now?"

Wadus stopped, lay on his belly, and tried to laugh but the pain in his ribs would not allow it. He thought, "Somehow I've got to get that man a compass." He then replied, "Face the back of your cell."

"O.K. man, now you try to sleep, you hear."

Wadus hoped his guess as to the direction of Mecca was correct. He eventually found the lavatory, pulled himself to his knees, and washed the open wound over his eye. He found the toilet paper and while pressing the wound together applied some damp paper to it. After some time he was able to locate the cot and raised himself onto it. He thought of Ms. Clark and of her beauty. His exhausted mind, and damaged body, carried her image into sleep.

Governor Trout entered his office early the following morning as he was eager to study the file of the inmate who had attacked his child. He was furious when he read the man had been convicted of two counts of assault with a deadly weapon. However, as he read on his anger diminished and he became bewildered. He reread the inmate's record several times and the account of the accident and trial. As an attorney himself he had much experience with lawbreakers, and court trials, but this case and the man he saw on paper were far removed from any experience he had known. Pressing a button he said, "Get me Warden White at Central." A few minutes later the Warden was on the phone.

"Good morning, Governor. I'm very sorry about what happened and I pray your daughter is O.K.."

"Yes, thank you. Warden, I want this incident to be completely off of the record. It will have disastrous effects on my child if the news media gets wind of it. It would make her life impossible, in school and everywhere else."

"Yes sir, I understand. I agree and will cooperate fully."

"Now about the inmate."

"Sir, he is in solitary confinement, and I intend to have him remain there for sometime."

"That's your decision to make. I will be frank with you, Warden at first I was extremely upset with both Ms. Clark and with you. However, I have just completed a close examination of this man's record, his crime, the trial, and his sentence. Now the only feelings I have are my concerns for my daughter. I must say I am somewhat confused and can certainly understand why you would think this inmate was completely safe but the fact is he attacked my daughter. It just doesn't seem to fit his profile."

"Sir, I have dealt with inmates for many, many years and I do not understand how I could have been so wrong about this one. But obviously I was, and I am deeply sorry."

"Thank you Warden. I will send his file back tomorrow. Good bye."

That night the Governor went to Debra's room where he found his wife. He held his daughter, as she cried, and assured her everything was fine and she need never to fear the inmate nor anyone such as him again. After his daughter had cried herself to sleep he and his wife went to their bedroom and he handed her the file on inmate 204. After carefully studying it she looked at her husband as if expecting some explanation and clarification. The Governor said, "I know, I can't believe what I read either."

The following day after the incident Debra had confided her secret to her close friend Kelly. Hearing the true account Kelly reacted with horror. "Debra, how could you do such a terrible thing? Do you hate that man that much? What has he ever done to you? God, Debra, he's already in prison! How could you?"

"No, I don't hate him, I just thought it would be fun to play a joke on him. Besides, I might even get a little attention from my mom and dad, they never have time for me anymore."

"You don't really seem to realize what you have done. God, Debra, I didn't know you were that kind of a person! I don't know if I want you for a friend?"

The two young girls talked several more times during the day, and by the end of that school day Debra had begun to understand the seriousness of her "joke."

The realization of a conscience is always traumatic and is an unusually heavy burden for a young mind. This burden grew heavier, and heavier, day by day, for this young adolescent girl. Mrs. Trout became more and more concerned as she held her daughter as she cried herself to sleep each night. She and the Governor began to wonder if more had not taken place in that bathroom than their daughter had told them. They were in agreement it was definitely time to seek professional help, however, the child's nuclear conscience exploded on the eleventh evening following the incident.

That night, Tom Trout held his daughter tightly as she wept. He had said, and done all his frightened mind could think of. Suddenly Debra broke lose, "Dad, I'm an awful person, and I know you and mom hate me!"

"Oh Baby, no—no—no, don't say such a thing, please. We love you more than ever!"

"You don't understand Dad, I can't stand this any longer!" Many terrible pictures raced through both parents minds and then Debra proclaimed, "No, no, you don't understand! I lied! I lied! I lied about Wadus! I tore my own blouse, I screamed, I lied, I lied, I lied, just to make it look like he attacked me! He never touched me, he was just cleaning and I slipped in the bathroom and closed the door. He was so afraid, and on the spur-of-the-moment I just decided to play a joke on him. I really didn't mean to harm anyone! Oh Dad, I can still see his face when they dragged him out the front, he just looked at me, he never said a word. Oh please forgive me."

The Governor could not believe what he heard, could not speak, and just held his posterity for some time. After she calmed somewhat he said softly, "Oh Baby, my Baby, don't worry Baby, Daddy's here and I'm not angry with you! Dad will take care of it and it will be all right. After all, what are Governors for? Thank you for telling us the truth; it took a lot of courage, I'm proud of you." Mrs. Trout stood close by looking, listening, and wiping the tears that flowed down her face. After only a short time Debra ceased to cry, held her father's hand, and was soon sleeping soundly. The demon had been exorcised and the child's mind was at peace once again.

The Governor and his wife quietly left the room and as they stood in the hallway looking at each other Mrs. Trout said, "Tom, that poor man, what are we going to do? That poor man! He never spoke, never denied anything! Oh my God, Tom what are we going to do?"

"Debra will be fine now. Honey, stay close to her, I have to go somewhere." He stopped his wife's question and said, "Don't worry, everything will be taken care of, I'll be back in an hour or so."

Governor Trout hurried to his office in the mansion and rang the number of Warden White's home. It was nine p.m. as the Warden responded, "Hello."

"Warden, this is the Governor. I'm sorry to bother you at this hour but there is an emergency that will not wait until morning. Meet me at Central in twenty minutes. I am on my way right now."

Chapter 12

The Power To Protect
"Conscience is a sacred sanctuary where
God alone may enter as judge." Lamennais

Warden White turned on the flashing lights of his state vehicle and raced toward Central Prison. He was very confused and could not imagine what had happened at Central that would have provoked such a call from the Governor. He would have been notified himself if there were a riot, fire, or major problem. He slid the auto to an abrupt stop in front of the prison and sat observing the area. He saw nothing unusual and this further peaked his curiosity. As he approached the main entrance a state patrol unit sped up and stopped. The Governor quickly exited the vehicle and walked to the Warden.

"Warden, let's go to your office." Within minutes they were alone in the Warden's office, and the Governor continued, "Warden, this could not wait until tomorrow. My daughter, only minutes ago, told her mother and I she had staged the attack on her and the inmate had done nothing!"

"What!"

"That's right. I guess she just thought it would be some type of practical joke and did not realize until later the seriousness of what she had done. Her conscience has put her through hell the last ten days. She confessed this to us, and I immediately called you. Now, I want to do whatever I possibly can in order to make this right and, if possible, to make it up to the inmate. He doesn't deserve or need this."

"Sir, we almost had a riot here the evening he was brought back, and his cellmate was placed in solitary shortly afterwards. They both are still there. What do you suggest I do to make this just go away?"

Governor Trout noted the tone of the Warden's statement and the implication you could not just erase such an injustice as if it had never happened. Yes, the man was an inmate, but he was also a human being.

"I realize what has been done can't be undone, however, I want you to do the following. If anyone ever asks it's an executive decision and I will take full responsibility. Now, have you seen or talked with the inmate?"

"No sir, I have not nor has anyone else."

"I want him brought to this office immediately, right now."

"Yes sir. Sir what about the other inmate, 204s' cellmate?"

"Return him to his cell immediately."

"Yes sir."

The Warden summoned an officer, gave him the orders, and then he and the Governor waited silently.

Wadus Strickland, inmate 204, had spent eleven days and ten nights in solitary confinement. He had endured his physical pain as well as the silence and darkness without complaint. He had been able to whisper to Mohamet from time to time and came to understand what a luxury communication with others was. He spent hours in deep and concentrated thought of life, death, love, worth, integrity, religion and values. He reviewed, remembered, and mentally saw every detail of every experience he had come to cherish with Ms. Clark. He saw her beautiful hair, eyes, sensual body, smelled her fragrance, and could feel her touch. He thought over, and over, of the questions she had asked him that wonderful day in her office. "Who are you? What are you?" He did not know the answers. He did not know but did know a strangeness had descended upon him following the accident. He could almost see the mind, and soul, of others. Maybe the Indians were right, maybe the Man Above does "touch" certain ones from time to time setting them apart from all others in order to work His will? He fantasized again about how wonderful life could have been "if" he, Jamie, and Trina, could have loved each other in his small kingdom by the sea near Sunset Beach. He saw his small cottage, his sanctuary, and the peace he had known there. He thought of Debra Trout and felt sorry for this child.

Wadus Strickland was not the only person in his world who had the gift. On the morning after he had been taken back to Central Ms. Clark entered the kitchen for coffee. Her eyes were red from the many tears she had shed the previous night. She poured a cup of coffee, but did not lift it, and stood gazing into the cup as if in a trance. She quickly turned and left the kitchen, leaving the coffee untouched. There were several comments from the staff as Mrs. Clara walked over, picked-up the cup, and left the kitchen. Mrs. Clara entered Ms. Clark's office and found her sitting at her desk with her head in her hands. She was crying. Mrs. Clara closed the door, walked over, put the cup on the desk, went around and wrapped her big arms around the weeping white woman.

"Shssssssssssss now, yo hush now chil! Yo ain't got nothin ta be ah cryin bout." Ms. Clark turned and embraced this grand old black lady as a small girl often clings to her mother when hurt and afraid. Mrs. Clara continued, "Now yo listens ta me chil cause I knows thangs, an I knows Snowball ain't done what dey say he's done."

Ms. Clark quickly looked upward into the wise and beautiful face of the elderly black lady and asked, "How do you know that Mrs. Clara?"

"I jus knows." So, Mrs. Clara began to tell this sophisticated, educated, white woman of a world she had not been taught of in college and never knew existed.

"I growed-up in da low-country of South Carolina, near Charleston. My mammy and pappy woe po, but good peoples. Dey wuz forteen of us younguns. My grand mammy and grand pappy had been slaves on one of dem rice plantations at one time. Well anyways, when I wuz jus ah little thang dey wuz dis old Black Gullah woman dat live by herself not to fer away. Somehows she took alikin ta me, din't lik most, she din't, and most wuz real fraid of her! She spoke dat Gullah talk an knowed thangs bout folks way back in time. She made ah bunch of dem potions, yeah, an could do conjuring. I seed her conjure da worts off ah mans' hands' dat wuz covered wid'em.

90

She all da time talk bout haints an used gouper-dust ta throw spells onto folks, an ta cure dem of bad spirits. She had ever thang painted blue round dat old shack, claimed hit heped keep da haints away! Dat old Gullah woman said she seed somethang in me, an dat I had da gift ta see thangs mos can't see. She kep me down dey a lot an school me in some of dem Gullah ways. I din't thank too much bout hit fer a lot of years but shore nough dey come ah time when I begun ta see thangs in peoples, an feel thangs bout'em dat onlyest ah few others is able ta. Chil dat fust day Snowball walked in dat kitchen I seed hit in dat man! He had da gif to! Wuz lik somthang white round him, minded me of snow. Yeah, I seed hit fo shore, dats why I calls him Snowball! Now cordin ta dat Gullah woman dat means ah good oman an dats why I tells yo dat Snowball ain't done dat ta dat chil! Hit ain't in hem ta do such, no sir, not fer one mimute hit ain't! So chil yo hush-up an wipe dem eyes clean. I knows yos got feelins fo Snowball an yo ain't ta worry no mo bout hem doin dat thang cause he din't! Trust in da Lawd chil, everthang gonna be put right! Trust in da Lawd!"

Ms. Clark stood-up, looked into this good lady's eyes, and said, "Oh Mrs. Clara, I love you! Thank you so much." She embraced Mrs. Clara again and said, "You will never know how much what you have said means to me. I feel as though a great burden has been lifted from my mind."

"Dat's good chil. Now, yo finish dat coffee, I is got ta see what dat foolish Shawna been doin since I been outta dat kitchen!" She left Ms. Clark to meditate on the wisdom, and love, she had just been shown by this beautiful old black lady.

The officers unlocked the doors of each cell and two escorted Mohamet back to cell 101 without any explanation as to why. The other two officers took inmate 204 to the Warden's office. Wadus had attempted to keep himself as clean as possible under the circumstances. He washed all his private parts and treated his wounds as best he could, however, his appearance was still of a beaten man who had been exiled for many days. Governor Trout was not prepared for the picture he saw as Wadus was led into the Warden's office and stood before them.

The Governor jumped to his feet and ordered, "Get this man a chair!"

Wadus sat down and leaned to the left as he held his arm close to his injured ribs in obvious pain. The Governor slowly walked around the chair where the inmate sat. The wound over the eye had begun to heal but looked terrible. The swelling had disappeared but the trauma of the blows was still very visible in shades of dark colors. Wadus sat and silently looked downward.

"What happened to you?" Wadus did not look-up, nor did he speak, and slightly shook his head as he held his arm to his injured ribcage. The Governor looked at the Warden, then at the guards, and back to Wadus and asked, "Do you know the names of the officers who did this to you?" Wadus shook his head indicating he did not. "Can you identify them?" Wadus nodded indicating he could indeed identify the officers who had beaten him.

The Governor turned to the Warden and said with the authority of his position, "I want all the guards in that section in this office right now!"

Warden White summoned the officers; there were eight. They entered the office and were told to line up to the right facing the seated inmate.

"Now, look at these officers and point out the ones that did this to you!" Wadus slowly turned his head and starting with the first officer looked each in the face for several moments. He turned back, lowered his head, and was silent.

Governor Trout waited briefly and asked, "Well, which one, or ones, beat you?"

Wadus turned slowly, looked coldly into the Governor's eyes, and spoke for the first time since entering the office. "You asked me if I could identify them, not if I would!"

The shocked Governor responded, "Don't be afraid, I promise you you don't have to be. They will not only not work here any longer but may well go to jail themselves. I give you my word, I will see that these men are punished to the strict maximum of the law."

Wadus looked back again to the Governor, nodded, and said, "I'm not afraid, and yes sir, I know you have the power to punish these men severely and would do exactly that. You have that power. I sir have a greater power. The power to protect them. They are, like everyone else behind these walls, only what society has made them. The society, sir, which you help to govern! Who has the power to punish that society? I choose to protect these men from your society, the society that made them what they are!"

Upon hearing these words heads snapped toward each other in total shock. The officers, especially the two who had beaten the inmate, could not believe what they had just heard. Governor Trout sat down slowly as if tired and studied the inmate thinking of what he had just heard. He then looked at the Warden and with a tired wave of his hand indicated the officers should be dismissed. Warden White ordered them to return to their duties.

As the officers left the office and walked down the hallway one of the guilty officers said to the other in a very low voice, "How the hell ya figure that dumb bastard?"

The officer spoken to whirled, grabbed the first officer, and slammed him into the wall and held him securely as he said, "No, you're the dumb bastard! You just don't get it do you! We didn't just get our asses kicked, we got our whole lives kicked, by a man who was helpless, and we beat the hell out of! He kicked the hell out of what we are, how we think, what we do for a living, how we treat other human beings, how we fucking are! Don't talk to me anymore, and if I ever see you raise that stick to another man, without real cause, I'll help him stomp your sick ass!" He released the officer and walked away. This officer would never again hit another inmate nor see them with the same perspective. He would never be the same man who had walked into the Warden's office expecting to lose his job and possibly sent to jail. He became not only a different man on his job, but a different man with his wife, his children, and in his community. He was to have a great impact upon the attitudes of many of the other officers. He constantly reminded himself he owed it all to a small man whom he had beaten, for no reason, but had chosen to protect him.

Governor Trout broke the silence, "Wadus, just what in the hell kind of man are you? You think you're Gandhi, St. Peter, maybe Jesus himself? Just what in the blue-perfect hell are you? You never denied attacking my daughter, you never said a damn word, why didn't you?"

"How is she sir?"

The Governor leaned back, shook his head and said, "Damn, you're something else. She's fine now. She told us tonight what really happened that afternoon and it's a great burden off her mind. This is the first night she will sleep without crying most of the night."

Wadus showed a slight smile and said, "That's good news, sir. I'm glad to hear it. Sometimes we're taken into deep waters not to drown us, but to teach us how to swim. Your daughter has learned how to swim sir."

"From the looks of you, you were the one who was in deep water."

"Oh, these wounds will heal, it's the wounds on the inside that sometimes never heal."

"Well, I'm not gonna sit hear and discuss philosophy with you, not that I wouldn't like to, but it's late and I'm exhausted. Hellfire man, you know, maybe I should make your next work detail over at the university. You could be professor 204, right. Wrong, you're coming back to the mansion as soon as you're able. I have my selfish reasons. You can drown or learn to swim Mr. Sage. The Governor turned to the Warden and said, "Have him placed in the infirmary and given whatever care he needs even if it means sending him to a local hospital with a twenty-four hour guard. When he is able I want him back at the mansion cleaning again. Just as soon as possible."

"Yes sir." An officer was called and inmate 204 was taken to the prison infirmary.

The Governor prepared to leave and said, "Thank you Warden White, I hope you feel as relieved as I do. I'm looking forward to some peaceful sleep for a change." He and the Warden left and went to their homes.

Once at the mansion the Governor looked in on his daughter. She slept the sleep of a newborn child. He joined his wife in their bedroom and related the events that had taken place at Central. Grace Trout was mystified, listened intently, and had many "why" questions her husband could not answer. She said, "Tom, I'm so ashamed of myself. The things I've said about him, the things I've thought about him, and I feel so strange about this man."

"Strange! Believe me honey, this is one strange man. You should have heard the lecture he gave me when I wanted to punish the officers who had beaten him. Sitting there all beat to hell, looking like he'd been caught by death and thrown back. I swear I haven't been talked to, or affected, like that since I was in high school! He's certainly not impressed by titles or positions, or at least not by mine. Grace, he is strange, he's in a different dimension. I feel it and somehow respect it, but it is one I have never known. Well, believe me when I say he will not fault you, it doesn't seem to be in his nature. I don't know what he is, or what he thinks he is, but I know he is coming back here as soon as possible."

"Is that a good idea, considering the way it may make Debra feel?"

"Yes, the best, because she'll have to face and confront what she did and then it will be over. She did wrong and we haven't raised that child to run from her problems. She proved that tonight. If she doesn't face this, it will be with her for a very long time, maybe forever."

Grace Trout agreed with her husband's logic. They held each other more tightly than they had for years and both enjoyed a night of peaceful sleep.

The mansion staff was unaware of the events of the past evening. After breakfast the Governor did not immediately leave, but went to his office. He rang for Ms. Clark whom he had avoided for many days. She reported fearing she would be admonished further. The Governor told her to close the door and have a seat. She was certain she was about to be dismissed as the mansion supervisor. Her heart began to race as the Governor cheerfully related what had taken place, and that Wadus would be returning as soon as possible. The tears made her bright eyes glisten, and she struggled not to show her boss the inner joy she felt and tried desperately to keep from bursting into uncontrolled weeping. The Governor concluded by saying, "I just wanted you to know what happened and also to apologize for the harsh things I said to you. I am truly sorry Ms. Clark."

Ms. Clark went directly to Wadus's favorite place and people. She poured herself a cup of coffee and tried to restrain her joy but could not. She walked over to Mrs. Clara, looked into her big round face, and bursting into tears she exclaimed, "Wadus is coming back; he didn't do it!" She embraced Mrs. Clara and wept as this fine lady patted her on the back saying, "Now, hush chil, I told yo everthang wuz gonna be alright." The smell of happiness once again blended with the other pleasing aromas of the kitchen, and there were shouts, many comments, and, of course, dancing by Shawna.

Trina Clark returned to her office, closed the door, and sat at her desk. She looked at the pimples on her arms and feeling an orgasmic rush, said to herself, " Mr. Strickland, it's a good thing you aren't cleaning in here right now. I'd lock the door myself. Probably for the rest of the day."

Chapter 13

THE GEEK

"Youth! Youth How buoyant are thy hopes;
they turn like marigold, toward the sunny side."
Jean Ingelow

Inmate 204 remained in the infirmary for the following nine days and, because of the Governor's instructions, was afforded the best care Central was able to provide. His ribs healed and the bruises and swelling disappeared, leaving only a scar over the left eye as the only visible evidence of physical contact.

Mohamet was anxious for his cellmate to return and wasted no time in getting answers to all of the prison rumors of recent days. Wadus told him of the Governor and the events that had taken place in the Warden's office. He was primarily concerned that Wadus would be returning to the same work detail at the Governor's mansion.

"Man, you keep on working there till something just as bad is gonna happin again. If I was you I'd just walk-off, then they'd bring you back here for shore. You better off in here; I told you about them people, you can't trust'em."

"There are some really fine people there, I enjoy seeing them, I've missed them. As for the child, I do think she will be different in the future, and if so, what happened to me is worth it for her sake."

"There you go talkin crazy again. Why didn't you tell dat Governor who them bastards was dat beat you? He done told you he'd fire'em. Maybe even lock their asses up. Now, nothin gonna happen to'em and they just gonna beat somebody else with them sticks."

"Maybe not. At least I'm pretty certain about one of them."

"Why?"

"When I looked at each of them closely I saw something. Both of them were afraid, but I saw something more than fear in one of them. I saw a light from him that everyone doesn't have. It was as though that light wanted to be let out and was the real person and not the one who had beaten me."

"Man, I don't know what you talkin about."

"I really don't either, but from time to time it seems I can almost see what someone's soul really is. I saw that in you Mohamet."

"Say what?"

"That's right I did, are you the same man who hit and threw me around this cell, who wanted to kill me for being white, who could not read his Holy Book, who wanted to be alone all of the time? Are you that man today Mohamet?"

"I admits I've changed some but I is still Mohamet Kabul."

"Yes, but a better one, a stronger one, a thinking one. That reminds me, the night they brought me back you purposely got yourself sent to solitary. Was that thinking?"

"Man, I done told you about that."

"Look Mohamet, I love you like a brother, and it makes me proud to think you care enough about me to do that, but listen to me. You are a very young man, a good man, a different man than they put here years ago. I want you to start thinking about yourself outside as a free person. Think of all you never had and now could have. Think about cutting your time and not adding to it. I see you outside, you will be outside."

"Man, I ain't got nowhere to go if I was let out, plus nobody gonna hire ah ex-con. I couldn't make a living."

"Don't even think about those things; they will be taken care of, trust me."

Wadus was glad to be with his friend and they talked long after the lights went out. He looked forward to the next day with great anticipation, for he would see his friends and Ms. Clark.

He arrived at the mansion just before eight a.m. the following morning. Going around he entered the kitchen. All stared briefly and with shouts, laughter, and welcome comments, came to greet inmate 204. Mrs. Clara arrived with a cup of coffee and one of her fresh buttermilk biscuits, she said, "Snowball, sits down at dis table an eat dis biscuit, hits good fo yo. We's missed ya Snowball."

Wadus was extremely grateful for this uncharacteristic show of concern from the martinet of the kitchen but had always known her heart was even larger than her body. He said, "Thank you, Ms. Clara, I've thought about these night and day since I was here."

Shawna's rock and roll music was still present, and with artistic movements she circled him, hugged him, and said, "Wadus, my main man, I never missed a man so much, let alone a white dude. Are you ready to boogie Baby?"

"No, Snowball ain't ready ta do no boogin, and gal yo git yo little butt back ta work." Shawna laughed, winked, and shagged back to her chores.

Wadus had been at the table about ten minutes when the door opened and Ms. Clark entered. She was especially beautiful this particular morning and was noticed by all present. Wadus rose as she approached the table smiling. He could not take his eyes from her face as she extended her hand and said, "Welcome back Wadus; we have all missed you."

Wadus took her soft hand as if holding a delicate flower and replied, "Thank you Ms. Clark."

"When you finish your coffee the Governor would like a word with you before he leaves."

"Yes ma'am."

Ms. Clark said, "Good morning all," and left the kitchen. Wadus left shortly and passing through several large rooms where he assumed the Governor would be finally saw him, Mrs. Trout, and Debra.

They were waiting for him and said, "Good morning."

Debra spoke first and said, "Wadus, I'm so—."

Wadus extended his arm and with a finger almost touching her lips stopped her and said, "Shsssssssss, I know Honey, everything's fine. I forgave you before I was out of the door."

The Governor and Mrs. Trout, looked at each other with surprise and approval

"Did they punish you a lot?"

"Not too much Honey, oh they wouldn't let me watch T.V. for a few days, I couldn't use the library or recreation area, and I was restricted to my room for awhile."

"Really!" Looking at the scar over his eye she asked, "How did you get that scar?"

Wadus touched the scar as he said, "Oh that, I think I ran into something."

Debra was extremely happy and relieved and said, "Well, I've got to get to school. Bye Mom, bye Dad, bye Wadus" and she hurried to her waiting transportation.

Mrs. Trout extended her hand and spoke first, "Wadus, I'm so very sorry for everything and thank you for the way you handled this. You're quite a diplomat. I'm sure everything will be fine now." Wadus shook her hand and just nodded. She said good bye to her husband and made her way up the long stairway.

The Governor shook Wadus's hand and repeated, "Thank you." He left the mansion for his capitol office.

After that day Wadus would most often refer to Debra as "Honey" as if she were his own little girl. In the weeks and months that followed she grew more and more attached to this inmate, housecleaner, man she had falsely accused, and person who would listen to her. He became her confidant, secret sharer, and friend. Wadus returned her attention with fatherly love and came to look forward to her enthusiastic arrival after school each day. He played games because it made him feel good. He would get someplace out-of-sight. When she arrived and did not immediately know where he was she would begin calling, "Wadus, Wadus, where are you?" Upon finding him would exclaim, "Oh there you are, you won't believe what happened at school today." She would proceed to tell him every detail about her day, who said what, what boy she thought was cute, what teachers were "geeks", and on and on. Wadus would just listen as he cleaned, never criticizing, but occasionally asking, "What do you think about that?" in order to cause her to think about something he considered important. Wadus knew adolescents don't really tell adults things in order to receive advice, and wouldn't follow it anyway. They share their thoughts and problems with adults who will just listen with concern. She would often bring her friend home after school, and on those days it was double the chatter, double energy, double questions, and double joy for Wadus. There were some topics he would not discuss with the girls and would always say, "I think you better ask your Mother about that." They would giggle and call him "old fashion."

Debra arrived home crying one afternoon and ran straight to her room. This greatly troubled Wadus and he hurt to think something was serious enough to cause her tears. He wanted to go to her, but thought he had better leave it to her parents.

He later learned students had received report cards that day and Debra had failed social studies. To her it was as if she had failed life, her parents, her friends, and there would never be any joy in her future. The following day Wadus heard Mrs. Trout calling him and replied, "I'm in the great room ma'am."

"Wadus, the Governor and I were talking late last evening, and we thought of you."

"Really, how so ma'am?"

She explained Debra's failure in social studies and how they had thought of ways to help. She asked, "Now, don't you have a teaching degree Wadus?"

"Yes ma'am."

"Any post-graduate work?"

"Yes ma'am. I have a Master's Degree in education."

"What subjects did you teach?"

"Many different ones over my career but mostly European Studies, Global Studies, Sociology and Psychology."

Mrs. Trout looked silently for a few moments and remembered noticing some of these facts in the file her husband had shown her on this inmate. She said, "And we have you cleaning house. I have noticed how fond Debra is of you, and it occurred to me that you might be able to help her."

"Anyway possible ma'am."

"Do you think you could help her with her social studies after she comes home each day?"

"Well ma'am, if I have the time, and it can be worked-out. I mean she is in school all day and then comes home to start all over immediately without any time to relax, that can be very stressful ma'am."

"Your cleaning duties can easily be altered. Will you do it?"

"Of course ma'am, I mean I'll be glad to try"

"Wonderful, you start tomorrow." She turned, walked away and left Wadus to ponder upon this new responsibility. He just could not escape being a "teacher", even as inmate 204 the mansion house cleaner. He wondered if his soon-to-be student would accept his new role as teacher rather than listener? He did not wish to lose the rapport he had established with this young lady whom he had come to regard almost as a daughter. He tried to recall exactly what course was taught at the eleventh grade level. He had no way of knowing what this child did, or did not, know. Many academic questions troubled him.

The following day Debra arrived after school and as usual went in search of Wadus. Her attitude was not the usual relaxed, and happy to see you one Wadus was accustomed to from her. She said, "Mom said you're going to start teaching me after school everyday. I didn't know you were a teacher; you're probably like that geek I have for history class. I hate history, I hate school, and I'll probably hate you for making me study more."

Wadus looked at her calmly, waited a few moments, and said, "Maybe I am a geek, whatever that is, and maybe you will hate me, but don't hate history. It's like saying you hate people, you hate yourself, you hate life. That is what history is, it's the story of life. I don't want you to study more, I want you to study less, but learn more. I can show you how if you want that. Honey, it's up to you, I will throw you a life jacket. Please don't throw it back. It is up to you." The young girl settled down somewhat and Wadus said, "Now, go get a snack and relax for a few minutes. I'll be up in thirty minutes, and you can introduce me to your textbook, O.K." She left to follow his instructions.

At four p.m. Wadus tapped on the open door of Debra's room and walked-in. She sat at her desk but said nothing as he sat in a chair next to the desk. He was relieved to see her textbook was *Men and Nations* by Hartcort & Brace, a world history text he was very familiar with. Wadus said, "Is this what's giving you all the grief?"

"Yes, I can't keep all those European names, and countries straight, it's too confusing."

"You are right, it is confusing. We are only going to deal with the important ones for now, the others will come to you over the course of your life."

She reached over and turned the radio on. It was the same music Shawna listened to in the kitchen. Wadus reached and turned it off as the young girl showed her anger and disapproval by saying, "Don't turn my damn radio off," as she turned it back on.

Wadus reached, turned it off again, and said, "One thing at a time, study first, relax second."

This on and off battle of the radio continued for several days accompanied by considerable profanity from Debra. Wadus knew he was losing this battle and sensed the mounting anxiety within this adolescent.

On the fourth afternoon Wadus reviewed Debra's classroom notes and tried to begin but once again had to silence the music. The young girl's frustration exploded and was visible as well as vocal. Jumping-up from the chair she shouted, "I can't learn this stuff; my mind's not on it."

"What is your mind on Honey?"

"I wish we were back home. I wish Dad had never become Governor. I wouldn't have to live this way. I could go to movies, dances, the mall, and for rides like all my friends do! Like normal kids do. I am as much of prisoner as you, and I hate it! All of my friends are trying to learn how to shag. That's a dance they do to beach music, and it's become very popular. When I do get a chance to go out I'll be the oddball geek girl who can't have a good time like all my friends. That's what's on my mind Wadus! If you knew something besides history you could really help and teach me to fuckin shag! But no, I have to be stuck here with some old geek while everybody else is having fun!"

She sat down and cried. Wadus first thought of the "f" word and how he seemed to be at constant war with that word. Then he thought of how true what the child had said really was. He finally became bold enough to accept a new challenge and said, "O.K. Honey, you've got a deal."

Debra's head snapped-up and she stared at him through her tears. She asked, "What do you know about dancing, especially shagging?"

"Honey I may be an old geek but the shag and those songs you listen to are old also. I danced and listened to them a long time ago. I still enjoy them and I do understand the shag is more popular now than ever."

Debra laughed and said, "I don't believe you! You can't shag!"

Wadus saw her intense interest and glancing at her clock said, "Honey, go downstairs real quick and tell Shawna to come up here for a few minutes. Now go—hurry, we don't have much time." She ran from the room as if the mansion was on fire, and Wadus looked through her collection of what he remembered as "beach music."

Debra ran into the kitchen shouting, "Shawna, Shawna!" and practically pulled her from the kitchen saying, "Come quick we need you upstairs, hurry, come on." Shawna was pulled along rapidly wondering what the emergency could possibly be.

As Debra pulled Shawna into the room Wadus sat looking at a tune he had picked out. He raised his hand and said, "Hi Shawna, ya'll close the door." Debra closed the door quickly, and Wadus continued, "Shawna, this young lady wants to see some shagging, let's show her some moves."

Shawna jumped into the air, clapped her hands and said, "Right on, get down my main man, let's do it."

"This number, "I'm a Girl Watcher" by the Okaysions went to number five in the nation in 1968 and remained there for nine weeks. The lead guitarist is a personal friend of mine, Donny Trexler. He plays a lot at the beach. I used to listen to him several times a week; he's real good. Let's try this one Shawna."

Debra put the tune into her player. Standing beside Shawna hip to hip, holding her right hand out front Wadus began a slow hip bump to fit with the rhythm. He lifted her arm over her head, spinning her around, and facing each other they shagged to the oldie with coordinated and synchronized feet and hand movements. Wadus spun Shawna using the female and then the male over the head turns many times. Debra sat on the edge of her chair, mouth open, eyes wide, as if witnessing some impossible phenomenon! Shawna was equally as shocked at the dancing talent of her partner and tried moves she thought he could not match. Wadus stayed with her and carried her into some she had never seen or done. The music ended and Wadus quickly sat down, as he tried to replenish his supply of oxygen. The two young girls jumped, clapped, laughed loudly, and made rapid comments. It had been many years since Wadus had seen such joyous enthusiasm in a young person, and he knew he had found a way to reach his student. If only he could muster the stamina to use it. Both girls were eagerly looking for another tune for more dancing but were stopped. With shortness of breath Wadus said, "No girls that's all for today, it's too late."

Shawna left for the kitchen and Debra was on Wadus verbally, "Wadus, that was awesome, nobody at school is that good. You're better than Shawna. Please Wadus, teach me how to shag, PLEASE. Will you please Wadus?"

"I might try, that is, if we can reach an agreement."

"I don't understand."

"I have to go, I'll think about it and we'll discuss it tomorrow, O.K., good night, Honey."

He left the room as Debra followed him to the front entrance and watched as he entered the prison van. He was no longer a "geek."

Chapter 14

The Contract
*"A teacher who is attempting to teach
without inspiring the pupil with a desire to learn
is hammering on cold iron."* Horace Mann

Wadus was not surprised when Debra arrived home earlier than usual the following day. She quickly located him and her eagerness to begin learning to shag could not be restrained. She said, "Come on, Wadus, I can't wait to start learning how to shag, come on now."

"Slow down, Honey, relax, Rome wasn't built in a day. Besides, there are some things to work out before we do start."

"Like what?"

"Go on up and I'll be there shortly." The young girl hurried to her room and Wadus arrived about ten minutes later. As he turned the radio off he said, "Sit down Honey, we have some things to talk about before we go any further with this dancing idea." Although impatient Debra sat in the chair at her desk and Wadus continued, "Now before anything goes any further we must have an agreement, a contract, so to speak. Do you understand what a contract is, Honey?"

"Yes, well sort of, it's something you sign."

"You are right; it is a legal document stating what each party will do and what they can expect from the other party. We are going to sign a contract."

"I don't understand?"

"Look, the primary reason I am here is to help you improve your history marks. I haven't been much use to you in that area, but I want to be. Your major concern at this point in your life is your social life and not your social studies, I remember those years myself. You want something, I want something, we must each agree to fulfill our responsibilities. Get a pen and sheet of notebook paper." Debra curiously, obediently did as she was told and Wadus continued, "Write this down. It is going to be our contract. I Wadus Strickland promise to, and will make every effort to, teach Debra Trout how to be as proficient as possible in performing a dance known as the "shag." Wadus allowed her time to get it written and added, "I Debra Trout promise to cooperate, obey, and listen to Wadus in studying history and will improve my grade in this subject. I further promise I will not ever use the "f" word and make every effort to eliminate profanity from my vocabulary altogether."

After she had written everything down she looked at Wadus and said, "Wadus, this isn't fair, I have to do all this just to get you to teach me how to shag?"

"Honey, there is nothing there that will not help you, and nothing there which will be easy for either of us. Very few things worth having are easy to acquire, and if they were everyone would be a big success. Learning anything is effort and practice, practice, and more practice! You must understand the seriousness of this before you sign it. If you sign, or if you do not sign, it is entirely your free choice."

"Wadus, are you saying if I don't sign this so-called crap, I mean paper, you will not teach me to shag."

"Exactly, nor will I try any longer to help you with your studies. It would be impossible. One more thing, if you do sign it, and break it, you will also break my heart. I will walk out, I am already in prison, they can only send me back to Central. No one will know about this contract except you and I, now think seriously before you make up your mind."

Wadus watched as this young adolescent mind tackled a major decision and attempted to think through it logically. It was stressful for them both and he was not certain of the verdict.

"Man, this is gonna be a lot of work. But, I've just got to learn how to shag, and if I don't get my history grades up Mom and Dad are going to get real nasty. O.K., Wadus, I'll sign it" She signed the agreement and passed the paper to Wadus. He signed, dated it, folded it up and put it into his pocket. He had signed many legal contracts over his adult life, land, homes, bank notes, teacher contracts and others, yet he felt he had just signed the most important one of his life thus far. It was a grand sensation.

Wadus knew it was too late to begin studying so he tried to answer as many of her energetic questions about shagging as possible. Like a father to his daughter he told of the fifties and sixties music, learning to dance, and stories of the beach he loved. He got so carried away he even told her of his small cottage near the ocean and of clubs such as Fat Harold's, the Spanish Galleon, the Pad, Poo's and numerous others. Suddenly he remembered the last time he was at Sunset Beach with his Jamie. He stopped, rose and said, "Good night Honey, God willing, I'll see you tomorrow," and made his way to meet the prison van.

That night as Wadus sat in cell 101 he looked at the paper he and the young girl had signed. He questioned his vanity and wondered if he could fulfill the promise he had signed. Was it possible? Did the time permit such grand objectives? His spirit was willing but oh how weak was the flesh. How fragile the mind, and tender the heart, was of his young student. His obscurity had disappeared, and he thought of the lack of mental stress when he was Jefferson's helper, or just a cleaning person, it was only physical labor. His night was restless as multiple scenarios of obstacles were spawned.

Mohamet had again admonished him saying, "Man you a fool! What them people gonna think when they hears that music and finds out you up there dancin with that young gal? They didn't axe you over to that big house to do no dancin— shore nuff not with the Governor's daughter. Well, one good thing, least your dumb white ass'll be back here before too long, that is if they don't shoot you first."

Wadus realized how valid these comments were and how real the possible danger also. He wondered "Why" these things

108

had not occurred to him and entertained Mohamet's thought that he might just be a "dumb white ass."

All of the following day he cleaned and thought, cleaned and thought, and was so preoccupied it drew the attention of Ms. Clark who asked, "Wadus, is anything wrong? Is something troubling you?"

"Oh no ma'am, why do you ask?"

Ms. Clark said in a whisper, "Dream of mine, I have purposely passed by you several times today and you have acted as though I was invisible. I feel like a silly school girl but these are the moments I content myself with each night."

Wadus loved to hear her voice and when she lowered it, and spoke with such open sincerity, it was as melancholy as the evening kooing of a mourning dove. He replied in a low voice, "Oh no, Trina darling, oh no. It's just that I have to start tutoring Debra this afternoon, and I'm as nervous as the first day I walked into a classroom over thirty years ago."

Ms. Clark reached over and gave him a slight, but nice, pinch on the arm and said, "Nevertheless, don't you ignore me cause I'll have you cleaning my office twice a day!" She winked and walked down the long hallway. Wadus watched her and wondered to himself about the male population in the Raleigh area? Were they all blind, did they think happiness was just a glandular condition, or did they simply not appreciate the grand total of God's artistic human work. Yes, he thought, males must have changed.

Debra arrived at 3:40 p.m. and Wadus was ready for he knew his time was limited and he had to maximize every minute. He explained the schedule to Debra. They would work on social studies for thirty minutes, the remaining time would be used for learning to shag. She wanted to shag first and study next, but he would not agree. He explained the importance of concentrated short periods of study as opposed to the negative diminishing returns of long cramming sessions. Study less, remember and learn more. This appealed to the student. They talked briefly about the textbook, he viewed her notes, made suggestions and was able to determine the instructor had just introduced the class to the Modern Era, 1500-present.

Wadus chose to begin with the rise of nation states during the sixteenth century. He wrote NIMAP in large letters and said, "Learn this word, it will be a tremendous mental guide. Now, name all of the Great Lakes for me."

"I can't do that, I know a couple but not all."

"Yes you do, all you need is someway to help you pull their names to the surface." He wrote the word HOMES on her paper and continued, "Each of these letters is the beginning letter of one of the Great Lakes. Now name them."

Debra looked at HOMES and slowly said, "Huron, Ontario, Michigan, Erie, and Lake Superior." She clapped, laughed, and said, "Wow, that's awesome, I'm smarter than I thought."

"You certainly are, Honey, all you need is a system to retrieve all that knowledge you have learned and will be learning. Now learn to picture the word NIMAP in your mind because each letter represents a major theme in world history from 1500 through this very moment. The first letter represents Nationalism, I is imperialism, M is for militarism, A is for Systems of Alliances, and P represents propaganda. Let's start with the N for nationalism." Wadus carefully explained that when a large group of people share the same language, religion, ethnic background, and culture they might come together as one nation. The strong pride, love, and patriotism which develops is a spirit of Nationalism. He explained this is what began to take place in Europe in the 16th century, before that time people had been very divided into small groups or states. His student paid attention and understood; it was a good beginning. It was 4:15. Debra put away the books and was eager to begin her first shag lesson. Wadus explained there would be many days without music as they worked through the basic steps. He found it awkward in his prison shoes on the carpet but, side by side, they began with the basic three-step movement. Three short steps forward, three backward.

"You know we really need a hard surface. I saw an old ping-pong table top in one of the buildings, I'll try to get it up here and we'll use it and then slide it under the bed. You will need a light pair of shoes with leather soles." So ended the first day of history and shagging, and Wadus hurried to meet the prison van.

The routine continued. Debra made good progress in accomplishing the academic objectives each day and little by little was beginning to feel comfortable with the basic movements of shagging. It had been almost two weeks without music, and Wadus finally said, "O.K. Honey, pick out a good tune and let's try what you've done to music." The eager young girl quickly did as told and rushed back to where Wadus stood on the ping-pong dance floor. He extended his right hand and she hers, establishing a rhythmic movement to the music they executed the basic shag steps toward, and away, from each other many times. As she came forward he raised her hand over her head spinning her back to face him in what is called the female turn. This new movement delighted the adolescent young female who insisted upon repeating it many times. Finally on one of the turns Wadus stopped abruptly and faced the door. Debra turned to see why. Mrs. Trout stood in the doorway watching with an amused but surprised stare. Wadus stepped over and silenced the music.

"Hi Mom, Wadus is teaching me how to shag."

"How to shag. What part of your history lesson is that?"

"Oh Mom, we study for the first thirty minutes and then Wadus teaches me to shag with the time he has left. Mom, can Dad have that truck pick Wadus up a little later each day? We need more time."

Walking over slowly and standing on the ping pong dance floor Mrs. Trout replied, "No honey, I'm afraid not." Inspecting the improvised dance floor she turned to Wadus and said, "So Wadus, you know how to shag do you?"

"Well ma'am, just a little."

"Mom he's great, he's even better than Shawna"

"Oh really, that is good. You know I always wanted to learn to shag, but we lived so far away from the coast and not many people in the mountains knew much about that type of dancing. Is this what younger people are doing now?"

"Yes, everybody at school wants to learn to shag."

Mrs. Trout looked once again at Wadus and said, "Well Wadus, what is the next thing about you that will shock me when I learn about it?" Before he could reply she asked, "How are the history lessons going?"

"Very good ma'am, Debra's trying very hard and is reaching her daily objectives. I hope it will be reflected in her class marks in the near future." He glanced at the clock, "Ma'am it is almost five, I have to catch my ride."

As he went through the door Mrs. Trout asked, "Wadus, may I join the shag lessons, that is, when time permits?"

Wadus was not expecting this but answered, "Why yes ma'am, by all means, please do."

After Wadus left Mrs. Trout continued to talk with her daughter and wished she had more such opportunities to spend time with her. Mrs. Trout, "You've really grown quite fond of that man haven't you honey?"

"Oh Mom, he's so-o-o-o cool, you should have seen him and Shawna shagging. I could not believe it! He knows all about the beach music and all those places down there. Mom, I really want to go to Myrtle Beach on vacation this year, can we please?"

"We'll see. Now tell me about what he's teaching you about history." Mrs. Trout tried to keep up with the conversation of the energetic teenager but mostly nodded and was thrilled to see her baby girl so happy and enthusiastic.

"Oh, he makes me study and learn for the first thirty minutes, but it goes so fast and he has ways to help you remember what you study. Like, you know, HOMES for the Great Lakes and stuff like NIMAP, if he was at school I wouldn't have failed." Mrs. Trout was lost but had no desire to restrain, or interrupt, and was content to enjoy her child whom she realized was rapidly growing up and would be away at college in only one more year. She remained for as long as possible and upon leaving thought many things. She realized she felt somewhat envious and a little jealous of Wadus. She was glad he was there yet wished Debra would bond with her, and her father, so openly and joyously as she evidently did with this inmate. She also realized the fact that he was an inmate made absolutely no difference to her daughter whatsoever. Once again she had cause to wonder, "What is it about this man? What is the charisma he possesses, I wonder?"

That evening in their large bedroom she related the events, and her feelings to her husband. Tom Trout felt sad and said, "Grace, I feel so bad because I'm not able to spend more time with my daughter and have a terrible fear I will look back and wish we had stayed in the mountains. A convict is becoming

112

closer to my little girl than I am. You say he can shag. That man's older than I am, what does he know about shagging?"

"Debra says he can and that he is good at it. I guess he's using it as some sort of incentive to get her to study her history and improve her history marks. It seems to be working. By the way, she even asked if you could have his evening ride come later. I told her no but you can expect to hear the request from her. She also wants to vacation at Myrtle Beach this summer; that seems to be the Mecca for shagging."

"My goodness, right now I'd rather be a good "shagger" than the Governor of N.C. I think I'd be closer and more respected by my daughter."

The lessons continued and days became weeks, weeks matured into months. Wadus stayed close to Debra's class topic each day and was able to clarify and reinforce what the teacher had taught each day. They proceeded through nationalism, imperialism, militarism, alliances, and propaganda as major causes of wars in modern times. They drilled and drilled on NIMAP as a mental roadmap for essays. They learned about the Commercial Revolution and she came to understand the fundamentals of capitalism, socialism, communism, and fascism. He emphasized the important royal families of Europe and taught her how to match the names with geography. Tudors in England, Bourbons in France, Hapsburgs in Austria, Hohenzollerein in Prussia, and Romanovs in Russia. She was instructed to remember the few outstanding monarchs in each family and not to become lost in trying to remember insignificant rulers who had little impact upon history. Mid term test time arrived and Wadus was confident his student was prepared. She only needed to believe this herself and to avoid becoming too nervous. He had seen good students create mental blocks and do poorly on tests even though they understood the material. The afternoon before he coached her in the smart way of approaching the multiple choice questions which she was unsure of. He pointed out that through an elimination process usually two of the four choices could be discarded, and the two remaining considered. If then unsure, guess, the odds were 50-50. A much better bet. Finally, he told her not to study that night, not to worry, and to get a good night's sleep. On his way out that afternoon he turned and said, "Hey Debra, you know it, I know you know it, and regardless of the mark you receive you're still the same person. I know you're A plus."

The following day was long and anxious for Wadus, and he was much relieved to hear the shouts as Debra burst through the entrance with joyous comments calling his name so loudly it could be heard all over the mansion. "Wadus, Wadus, I aced it, I aced it, where are you, I aced it! I know I did."

It was difficult for Wadus to reign-in this spring filly, however, he was eventually able to determine he had been correct in anticipating many questions, and events, which might be emphasized on the exam. For the first time this young girl was very anxious to receive her history grade, but realized it would be several days.

They celebrated by devoting that day to dancing only, and there was extra bounce, movement, laughter and wholesome joy displayed by his young student. She fetched Shawna from the kitchen and the good times rolled! Wadus was happy, but exhausted, as he made his way to the prison van.

Chapter 15

A New Home

"It is better to hear the rebuke of the wise,
than for a man to hear the song of fools."
Ecclesiastes: 7,V5

Inmate 204 continued the daily routine to and from the Governor's Mansion and had increasing contact with the Governor and his wife. He enjoyed a subservient, but relaxed, relationship while in their presence. Nevertheless, he was always glad to return home to cell 101 and the company of his dear friend Mohamet Kabul. Mohamet continued his prison education and made more and more use of the limited library. He was extremely interested in theology but profoundly troubled as he explored the history and concepts of religions other than Islam. Wadus understood his deliemma having been reared in the strict Southern Baptist tradition of Robeson County, North Carolina. There were no other faiths, no other correct choices, no other proper ceremonies, and he had come to believe that Jesus himself must have been a Southern Baptist. It was comforting to know he had been fortunate enough to have been placed upon the only true path to God's Kingdom. This comfort quickly ended upon his entrance into college. Like Mohamet, he studied, and learned, of other religions. Words such as Jewish, Catholic, Protestant, Moslem and Hindu were no longer just "words" but were peoples and philosophies! Were so many millions wrong? He was astonished as a freshman college student to learn A.D. did not mean "after death" and was frightened to realize how limited his education had been. He had grown up in a small southern community that was deformed by cultural incest. Outside ideas, people, places, religions, and even foods were taboo. He laughed as he remembered the first time he ate in a restaurant. He was in the eighth grade, the first pizza he tasted was his first year of college. He remembered those days when college, and golf, were exclusive privileges of the gentry. The laboring class, nor their offspring, were expected to aspire to either, and when one did seismic cultural shock rippled through the community. Yes, he understood his friend's concerns, listened to his questions, his thoughts, and tried to help him to reach a comfortable closure and validity of all major theologies. After all, God had only given man the intelligence to know He did exist and nothing more. Man was not intelligent enough to know, or understand what God is where He is, how He works, nor any of the other questions which have caused mankind to spawn so many different religions to explain what cannot be explained. Finally Wadus encouraged Mohamet to concentrate upon tolerance and the belief we all worship the same God. Mohamet continued to be stereotyped as Central Prison's lion but managed to stay free of trouble that would further damage his record.

The mansion housekeeper whom Wadus had replaced eventually recuperated and returned to her job. He assumed he would be restored to his original job as Jefferson's helper but he assumed wrongly. His chores now became more as butler than house cleaner, and he found himself answering the door, waiting on the Governor, his wife, helping in the kitchen, and tutoring Debra. As he went from kitchen to dining room during breakfast, and occasional lunches, his presence became routine. Eventually, the Governor, and Mrs. Trout, would even ask, "Wadus, what do you think," concerning some topic they were discussing. He would avoid giving an opinion most often, however, it got to the point he cautiously gave a short answer.

The Governor made every possible effort to be at the mansion near his daughter and wife as much as possible. Sometimes he would surprise Wadus, and delight Debra, by popping into the room for a brief visit during the history or shag lesson. He scheduled as many small meetings as possible in the mansion office and conference room. Wadus came to recognize the faces of state solons, politically, economically, and socially important persons. They never acknowledged his presence and assumed him to be another employed house servant.

Wadus began to be called upon to serve coffee, and refreshments, during some of the Governor's meetings. The first time he was called to the Governor's office there were four men present and the Governor. Wadus served all and silently listened to names, comments, and memorized faces. He noticed one did most of the talking and casually referred to the Governor as "Tom," the Governor addressed him as Senator. Wadus became even more observant, and curious, as the Governor finally said, "Senator Jacobs." He recalled the day Warden White had inquired if he knew a Senator Jacobs? Was this the same man? He was not sure but was positive this man was politically powerful in state politics. He was often in the mansion. After one such visit Wadus entered the office to collect the serving tray, cups, and glasses. The Governor sat alone as if in deep, uneasy, thought. He looked at Wadus and said in a depressed tone, "You know, more and more, I question myself and wonder why I ever wanted this job. I feel like a coon up a tree surrounded by a pack of hounds. Some of the stuff I'm asked to sign, and to endorse, I don't know about or understand. But, that's politics, you gotta play the game, right Wadus?"

"No sir, that isn't right!"

The Governor was not expecting to be disagreed with by this inmate and was shocked. He said, "You don't, why not?"

"Because you are not a coon up a tree! You are the Governor of the State of North Carolina. Yes, it's a great burden to know about everything you sign into law, and that you endorse, but that is what you promised the people of this state and not that pack of hounds."

"That's very idealistic Mr. Wadus, but the reality is that they are why I am here and will be why I am here if elected for a second term."

"Yes sir I know. Sir, please excuse my frankness, but you have a choice. You can be an outstanding one term Governor remembered by the people for making difficult decisions which hurt you politically but helped them, or you can be a two term Governor who just occupies this mansion and will never be remembered when you leave."

"O.K. let's drop it. Take your stuff away."

"Yes sir", and he left the Governor to his hounds.

The inmate had left the Governor physically but his words remained and their truths could not be ignored. The Governor thought how grand it would be to have an aid who, like this convict, had nothing to gain or lose and would state the opposing point of view. He said out loud, "Wadus Strickland, inmate 204, mansion house servant, tutor, protector of his assailants, shagger, former teacher, and whatever else I don't know!" The Governor nodded, slightly smiled to as if he had just received a brilliant revelation. Another dimension was about to be added to the life of inmate 204, a man who cared little for his own life.

In the following weeks Wadus saw the Governor early each morning but had usually been returned to Central by the time he returned to the mansion each evening. Several times Tom Trout had sat in his office late in the night and thought of inmate 204. He vacillated in reaching many decisions and longed for an honest unrestrained opinion. He thought of his daughter's request to have the van arrive later. He thought of possibly keeping the inmate at the mansion overnight but dismissed each as impractical and impossible to arrange.

Two days later inmate 204 was told to be in the Governor's office at 3:30, to remain there, and to serve refreshments when called upon by those present. He followed instructions, made preparations, and stood silently to the side of the large office as the meeting began. Wadus only responded as the participants held up a cup or indicated they desired something else. At 4:30 there was a knock upon the door that gained everyone's surprised attention.

The Governor looked at Wadus and said, "Get that please and tell them we are not to be disturbed."

Wadus did as told and on opening the door looked into the face of his student. She made no attempt to quietly state her position and said, "Wadus, what are you doing, you're supposed to be upstairs helping me, it's 4:30?"

"Shssssss Honey, your Father is having an important meeting and needs me in here."

"What? Tell him to come out here, I want to talk with him."

All inside were aware of the young lady's displeasure and tone as the Governor said, "Excuse me gentlemen," and went to the door closing it behind him said, "Debra lower your voice, you're not only interrupting an important government meeting, but you are embarrassing me."

"Big deal Dad, I don't care. Wadus is supposed to be helping me, and you have him down here. Don't blame me if I fail."

"We'll talk about this later, now excuse us."

Debra stormed away showing her wrath as only a teenager can as her father shook his head as he and Wadus returned to the meeting. The meeting dragged on, legislation, opposition, support, campaign funds, were discussed and at 5:15 there was another interruption. Wadus quietly whispered to the Governor the prison van had been waiting 15 minutes and the driver was very upset.

"He is is he, tell him to complete his route and return here, and tell him I said not to get the Governor "upset.""

This was done and the meeting finally ended at 7:15. Wadus hurriedly cleaned and gathered trays, cups, glasses, and ashtrays as all departed.

"Don't be in such a rush, besides you have already missed your dinner, make yourself a couple of sandwiches before you leave."

"Yes sir I will," as he thought of Mohamet and the opportunity to take him a special treat. He worried his cellmate might think him to be in solitary again and do something to damage his record.

The Governor intruded upon his thoughts and inquired, "Well Wadus, what did you think of the meeting?"

"Sir, I am not familiar enough with most of it to have an opinion."

"You must remember something! What stands out in your mind more than anything else which occurred here today?"

"Protocol sir."

"Protocol, what are you talking about, Debra's tirade?"

"Oh no sir, not that. I mean that all the men present, except one, extended you all the proper amenities and courtesy that your position as Governor of N.C. calls for. They referred to you as "Governor" and used "sir" in speaking to you. That one gentleman never said "sir" one time and referred to you as "Tom" not as "Governor.""

"Oh, you mean Senator Jacobs. Well, he's a very important and powerful man in the legislature and also the best campaign fundraiser in our party. I owe him a lot for helping me be elected to this office."

"I understand sir, but you are now the Governor. Is a state senator more important, and powerful, than the Governor?"

"Just what is your point?"

"Sir, every organization has a hierarchy of authority and each person must recognize the power figure above his position in order for things to operate smoothly. It seems to me that by not recognizing your superior authority one is actually saying he has equal, if not more, authority than you do. I mean sir, that listening to this man address you casually as "Tom", as well as the way he seems to dictate, I believe he sends out a psychological message to you, and all others present. That message is that you may be the Governor of N.C. but they should know it is he who really rules. I think that is why he calls you "Tom" and it's what I meant by protocol."

"I'm not sure about your observations, but I do admit he does exert his influence. You finish, get something to eat and catch your ride. I've got to go upstairs and face my greatest critic." Wadus left for the kitchen and the Governor for his daughter's room.

Governor Trout entered his daughter's room and found her sitting upright in her bed, arms folded, and doing some powerful pouting. He said, "Honey, I'm sorry you missed your lesson, I'll try not to use Wadus that time of day and besides you were able to enjoy a little break in your routine."

"Break! Dad, I can't believe you, break! That's the last thing I need, or want, especially at this time of year. The big school dance is coming up, and then the final exams not long after. I need Wadus for both. Besides, I asked you a long time ago to have him picked-up later, and you said it was not possible. Why was it possible today?"

After much apologizing, and feeling reasonably sure he had been forgiven, the Governor made his way downstairs toward the kitchen for like Wadus he had also missed dinner.

The Governor prepared himself a sandwich and as he was surveying this seldom visited part of the mansion began to explore. He followed the narrow hallway and turned on the light in the small storage room. Opening a door on the right side of the room he discovered a small restroom about eight feet by eight feet. There was a toilet and lavatory. He studied the small area carefully and stepped back into the storage room and took note of its size. He guessed it to be at least twelve by twelve feet. As he ate he continued to appraise both rooms he said out loud, "Well Debra, maybe these rooms are the solution."

The following morning Ms. Clark was called to the Governor's office.

"Ms. Clark, there is a small bathroom, and storage room, down the hall from the kitchen."

She was not familiar with the area but replied, "Yes sir."

"I want you, right away, to have a shower installed in the bathroom, and put some cheap tile on the floor. Better put a small vanity and cabinet in also. Then have everything in the storage room next to the bathroom moved someplace else. Paint both rooms, then furnish that room with a single bed, couple of chairs, and maybe a small desk. You got all that?"

Ms. Clark took notes rapidly, and finally asked, "Sir, is someone moving into that room?"

"I don't know Ms. Clark. I might just use it to hide from everyone now and then."

"Oh I see."

"Now I want this done ASAP."

Ms. Clark acknowledged his wish and left wondering about the true purpose of this project.

The following morning Ms. Clark found Wadus in the kitchen and said, "Wadus, show me the small storage room." Everyone in the kitchen watched curiously as Wadus led her away toward the room.

Shawna laughed and in a low voice said, "I sure hope Wadus gonna be safe in there, I better go check on him."

"Hush gal. Onlyiest thang yo gonna check on is dis kitchen work. I reckons Snowball kin takes care of hisself."

Once in the storage room Ms. Clark inspected the bathroom and said, "Wadus, the Governor wants everything in here moved someplace else. He's having a shower installed in the bathroom and a bed, chairs, and desk in here. I don't know what's gotten into that man. It looks like someone will be moving-in." She turned, smiled, and walked up and leaned face to face with Wadus. She looked into his eyes and whispered, "Mystery man, I just had a great fantasy. You are going to move-in here and stay at the mansion. I'm going to work late lots of nights, and when I come to the kitchen for coffee I'll be lured in here and repeatedly seduced by you. Could you make my fantasy come true?"

Wadus looked down, he could not resist what leaned against his body. The face, the eyes, the hair, and oh that delicious smell! He gently ran his hand along her soft neck and behind her head, slowly coming back to her ear, with one finger he circled the ear several times and then brought the finger slowly across her cheek. With a feather touch he traced her beautiful lips. She closed her eyes and taking the end of his finger into her mouth rolled her tongue around and kissed it. He leaned down and their lips lightly met. He slowly licked her lips with his tongue, then followed with soft spider kisses over them. Finally he pulled her hard into his body and kissed her passionately. He said, "Trina darling, we'd better get out of here before someone comes in."

"I know, just remember, someday I am going to make you pay dearly for this, and I'm adding much interest. So there, dream of mine." She refreshed her lipstick, wiped his lips with her handkerchief, and they re-entered the kitchen. As she left she said, "You may as well start moving those food goods into that other room," and she was gone.

Wadus began the relocation of goods and was troubled by the possibility of the impossible. Did this project have any thing to do with him; had Ms. Clark jokingly predicted his new home? He silently lectured, and scolded, himself for his lack of restraint, weakness of the flesh, and his desire for a dream walking.

The renovations were begun post haste and the Governor quizzed Ms. Clark daily. She informed him everything would be completed and furnished within the week. That day when time permitted he reached Warden White in his office at Central Prison. Both exchanged good mornings and the Governor then dropped the bomb. He said, "Warden, as you know, for many months we have had inmate 204 here each day on work detail."

"Has something else happened?"

"Oh no, no, well nothing like before. That incident has been forgotten by everyone. No, on the contrary, he has been a great asset to us all and actually this is the purpose of this call. The fact is that he becomes more and more helpful. The problem is his schedule. He arrives at eight a.m. and is picked-up at 5 p.m. We need him here before and after those hours."

"I see, what do you have in mind?"

"I would like him to start staying here overnight as much as possible."

"Governor, I don't know that I am willing to permit that. We would both be way-out on a limb, not to mention what certain persons and the media would do with this if it were to become public knowledge."

"I have considered all you have said, however, I want this man here, and I will take such a chance. If anything does go wrong all you need to say is you were ordered to do this by the Governor, and I will verify it. You have my word Warden; so, do we have a deal?"

"O.K. sir, it will be arranged. When do you want this to begin?"

"Tomorrow night; that should give you ample time to make the needed adjustments."

"Very well sir, but there is something I feel you need to know but it must be in supreme confidence and completely off of the record. I have kept what happened at the mansion completely confidential, now I ask you to do the same with this information."

"As you wish, what do I need to know?"

"Governor, almost three years ago about thirty minutes before inmate 204 arrived I received a telephone call from a Senator Jacobs. Do you know him?"

"Yes, of course, he's quite important in state government and we meet often."

"This senator asked me to put this inmate in with the most dangerous person in Central and to make his term much more difficult than is usual. For some reason it seemed he hoped the man would not live very long. Unfortunately I put him in with the worst inmate in this institution but, somehow, thank God, he not only survived but has had a great impact upon that inmate. I understand that man has protected him and continues to do so. The reason I tell you this is so you will be aware and cautious not to allow the senator to know who prisoner 204 actually is."

"Thank you for sharing this with me, and you are right, I did need to know this. Warden, were you ever able to find out why he asked you to do such a thing?"

"He claimed the inmate had violently attacked two young college kids and he requested it on behalf of them and their families."

"Yes I read his file, I know all about those 'innocent college kids' and what happened."

"Me too, I had the same thoughts, and frankly sir I don't see 204 as a criminal and I've had a strange feeling about him since the first time he stood in front of my desk."

"Yes, I know. Well Warden, all men in prison are not criminals and all criminals are not in prison. We live in a very imperfect world. O.K., I'll inform all here of the new arrangements, and thank you so much Warden White. Keep in touch, good bye."

Governor Trout added the warden's information to the thoughts expressed by Wadus concerning Senator Jacobs. He felt he was beginning to see things more clearly and realized he indeed needed to impress upon the senator the fact he was the Governor of North Carolina.

The Governor phoned Ms. Clark and informed her of the new situation and instructed her to advise Wadus. She was practically speechless, "Yes sir, Yes sir, good bye." She went immediately and found Wadus cleaning in the great room. "Wadus the Governor just called. Beginning tomorrow you are to stay in the mansion full time and not go back to Central each night. That room and bath was for you, I can't believe it, I just can't believe it. Isn't this wonderful?"

Wadus did not reply as he slowly sank into a large chair and stared at the floor. Ms. Clark had not expected this reaction and asked, "What's wrong Wadus? I thought you would be overjoyed."

"No Trina I'm not, my home has been Central Prison, cell 101 for nearly three years. My cellmate and friend is there. I'd rather stay there."

"I can't believe that, why on earth would you feel that way?"

"That cell is supposed to protect society from me, I feel it has protected me from society."

"Do you feel it protects you from me?"

"No, I don't ever want anything to protect me from you. It never could; you are with me every moment. If some miracle should allow it to be so, we would live in our own little cell, love, and protect each other. I am just afraid of my new home."

"Please don't worry, it hurts me, just think of the future. I do and everything becomes brighter."

The mood was very solemn in cell 101 as Wadus revealed his transfer order to Mohamet. He said, "Man I told you ah long time ago to just walk off and then they would put you back here for good. Now you done made them think they gotta have you there all th time. I probably won't ever see your dumb ass again."

"Maybe they'll let me come back occasionally, and I'll try to work out some way to call you. Who knows, maybe I'll get the Governor drunk and then get him to pardon both of us." Both men were able to laugh at this thought.

Chapter 16

The Party

"On with the dance! Let joy be unconfind'd;
No sleep till morn, when Youth and Pleasure meet."
Byron

Inmate 204 occupied his new quarters in the storage room and observed a paging phone had been installed in order to summon him at any moment. All were surprised, but glad, for the new house- guest. Debra was especially enthusiastic and thought she had been totally responsible. She made it very clear she would require more, and longer, dance lessons.

Tom Trout had been Governor of N.C. for three years and it was assumed he would run for, and easily be re-elected for a second term. This assumption was based upon keeping the support of the party hounds. He was to lose all very quickly.

Senator Jacobs entered the mansion office with urgency and began taking papers from his briefcase as he said, "Tom, I need you to sign these immediately so everyone can be given the go ahead."

Wadus stood, as usual, to the side waiting to serve if called upon. There were two other legislators accompanying the senator.

"What are these papers which so urgently need my signature?"

The senator looked surprised that he had been questioned and answered, "Oh Tom, it's nothing you need be concerned about, just some little highway project. We've already taken care of all the details."

As the Governor thumbed through the thick stack of papers he said, "Senator, this pile of details look pretty extensive to me, and I want some time to study them."

The senator was still standing and growing increasingly impatient with the Governor and replied, "Now look Tom, time is money, we don't have time. I need your signature on these papers."

Wadus saw Tom Trout become Governor Trout of North Carolina as he looked up quickly at Senator Jacobs and snapped, "Senator, I'll determine the time, and after I study this I'll also determine if they shall receive my signature, is that clear?"

Senator Jacobs was furious and said, "Tom you just made a huge mistake! Come on gentlemen we are finished here."

Wadus watched as the first two men exited but was again shocked to hear Governor Trout adamantly command, "Senator Jacobs." The Senator stopped and looked back as the Governor ordered, "Step back into my office for a moment." The senator did as ordered and approached the desk where the Governor sat. The Governor looked at Wadus and said, "Close the door," and it was done. The Governor sat for a moment looking coldly into the angry face of the Senator and then spoke, "Sit down Senator, I don't like looking up at a man when I'm talking to him." The Senator reluctantly sat. The Governor stood up and looked down at him as he put his hands upon his hips. He said, "Senator Jacobs, we need to get a few things straight once and for evermore. The first has to do with protocol. I highly resent you referring to me as "Tom!" Don't ever do it again as long as I am Governor of this State. You will address me with the dignity and courtesy this office requires. Secondly, in the future, do not expect my signature on any bills, legislation, endorsements, or anything else until I have had an opportunity to study them. Then I may, or may not, sign them. Do you fully understand me Senator Jacobs?" The Senator did not reply but slowly turned and looked at Wadus as if he regretted having had someone hear how he had been talked to and feared the story would spread. Governor Trout said, "Oh don't worry about him Senator, he's an inmate from Central, you might say he is the Governor's prisoner. Show him Wadus." Wadus opened the white jacket and pointed to the number 204 on the blue prison shirt. The Governor continued, "Yes his number is 204 and he is an inmate so no one will know what has taken place here today except us. He does however have a name, his name is Wadus Strickland." The Senator looked perplexed as if trying to recall where he had heard that unusual name. Governor Trout said "thank you Senator and good day to you!" Wadus opened the door to allow the senator to quickly depart. He turned back and met the Governor's eyes. Governor Trout smiled, "Wadus Strickland, I just became a one term Governor, but at least it feels good to finally be Governor. By this time tomorrow party leaders will be discussing who to run in my place next year, so all I need be concerned about is this next year and making plans to return home."

"Sir, I hope you will re-think what you just said."

"What do you mean?"

"Governor, it is true these political money hounds probably did enable you to become Governor, but the people of N.C. elected you. It will be those same people who elect the next Governor."

"You're not suggesting I should even consider running for a second term are you? That's insane."

"I think there's an opportunity here to capitalize upon some Machiavellian strategy, you know, "the end justifies the means."

"No, I don't see your point."

"I mean these men, the machine, the hounds, their money, picked you. They put you here because they assumed they could control you and it would be business as usual. However, you now have great power, power to say, I just allowed you to think I was your puppet. I am not. Now, I can be the Governor I want to be. The Governor millions of North Carolinians desperately need. You sir are now in a position to literally shock the hell out of the people, and even the nation, by beginning a truly Jeffersonian-Jacksonian era of reform."

Governor Trout had never seen his inmate so uninhibited, and enthusiastic. He listened carefully and then said, "Continue Wadus, it sounds like a fairy tale but an interesting one."

"I would need some time to really outline specific goals, but I can absolutely assure you the average working man, and woman, in this state would be surprised to see programs, and laws, which were truly designed to help them. I believe this is true across America and it is wrong. They should be furious when governments do not act for the benefit of the masses who elected them to do their will. The mass vote, the majority, of average N.C. citizens can put you in that chair for another four years, sir. I have great faith in this socio-economic majority, yes sir, you could not only win but start something which could make you one of the most outstanding Governors in this nation. Of course, the machine, special interest groups, big money, the hounds, will label you as mad and make your life miserable."

"Yes, I certainly agree with your last remark. Right now I have to study this so-called urgent highway bill." Wadus left the Governor but hoped he would reflect upon what had been said. The Governor did indeed think seriously of his position and millions of working class Carolinians, like his parents, Wadus had referred to.

Debra's final mark in social studies was eighty-nine, a B+, and she had made equal progress with her shag lessons. She became more and more coordinated, limber, and was able to follow when Wadus would surprise her with a new movement. Wadus learned Mrs. Trout had been spending many late evenings on the ping- pong dance floor being instructed by her daughter. Debra took pride in being able to "teach" her mother something, and her mother savored the joy of a greater closeness with her child.

Wadus missed the company of Mohamet and the daily ride, and sights, to and from prison. His typical day was not difficult but was long. He usually ate his dinner alone in the kitchen after everything had been completed for the day. His storage room quarters was adequate. Ms. Clark had included a dresser, mirror, a few pictures, and even a small radio. He had declined her offer of a small television and usually kept several books from the mansion library. Quite often he would be called on the mansion inter-com and requested to do something, or take something to the Governor's bedroom. He came to understand the Governor enjoyed a bourbon and water cocktail and Mrs.

Trout a glass of fine chilled wine. Debra would often request some snack, or treat, but most often it was an excuse to ask or tell him something really important. This girl at school said this, wears that, some boy was really a dream, another was a nerd and pestered her all the time, certain teachers were still "geeks", how much she looked forward to attending UNC, and how cool her mom was for trying to learn to shag. Wadus listened with occasional nods and comments such as, "Really," "that's interesting," or "oh, I know that must have hurt your feelings." He felt a nearness, and contentment, as he imagined he might have been listening to stories from his Jamie. She was now just a little older than his son would have been and Wadus wondered if his Jamie might have had a teenage sweetheart just as precious as this child?

Mrs. Trout informed Ms. Clark of a planned social event at the mansion. There would be fifty to sixty couples present. Cocktails would be served from 6:30 until 8:00, dinner from 8:15-9:30, followed by band entertainment and dancing. Ms. Clark informed Wadus his services and presence would be very much required. She was very amused at his obvious nervous reluctance and thought it quite humorous. She laughed and said, "Sweetheart, I'm not sending you to solitary confinement. It is just a social event at the Governor's mansion; important people, fine food, good entertainment, nothing to be frightened of." She left laughing, but Wadus did not share her laughter. He tried to imagine his duties and hoped whatever they would be would keep him isolated most of the evening. He reasoned it would indeed be so, no one would ever want him moving about such society in his prison shoes, trousers, and aging white jacket. Sure, everything would be fine, he would keep a low profile and try to stay out of sight.

The kitchen staff planned and prepared for this special social event and Wadus was utilized more than usual but did not mind. The day arrived and Ms. Clark demonstrated her expertise, and taste, in supervising every minor detail. The mansion was pristine, many baskets of flowers arrived, bars were stocked, glasses polished, and great quantities of food were cooked.

Ms. Clark; smiling with delight, approached Wadus around 12:30 p.m. as he did some last minute polishing in the great room where quests would first gather for cocktails. She said, "Wadus, I know you've been worried about tonight and that is why I've waited until now to tell you what I want you to do. Be at the front entrance to greet guests at 6:15 and—."

"What! Greet guests!"

"Don't be alarmed Baby, you'll be just great. Greet them, smile, collect their invitations, any apparel they want to check in, and direct them to the great room. After 7:00 come into the great room and help serve drinks. You may not be needed in serving dinner but will be needed to serve drinks during the dance."

He heard what she had said but could not believe it. "You're not serious, you're just teasing me, right?"

"No darling, I'm not, I'd never tease you."

"I can't believe you want me to greet anyone dressed in the clothes I have."

"That has been taken care of. You should start getting ready by at least 4:30. Now, I gotta go. See ya tonight sweetheart."

Wadus did as instructed and went to his room at 4:30. There were several boxes on the dresser and bed. He first recognized a shoebox and found a beautiful pair of light weight black shoes which were the correct size. Then a box containing black trousers, the waist and length were perfect. He further discovered a black leather belt, black socks, a black vest and a narrow red tie. Another box rendered a nice long sleeve shirt with pleats in front. Finally he opened a small box which contained Drakkar Noir cologne and a note. He read the note slowly, "My Dearest Wadus, these things are for you, from me, not the state. Having watched you so closely for so very long I am relatively sure they are the correct sizes, or at least, quite close. I have never enjoyed shopping for anything as much as I did for these few items. Just knowing they were for you gave me a feminine pleasure I have never experienced. I know you will be most handsome, probably too handsome. I love you, Trina." Wadus read the note several times. Shaking his head he viewed the gifts and thought, "These are very expensive gifts. How is this possible? How can such a beautiful woman, inside and outside, care for me? I am much older, a convict with no hope of a future. I can do nothing in return." He felt guilty and thought of what a wonderful treasure she would be for some eligible bachelor. Yes, men must have changed on the other side of the prison walls.

He showered, shaved, and dried his long silver hair. As he dressed he felt somewhat like a matador and carefully viewed every detail of his tasteful new outfit. Finally he tied a tight Windsor- Knot in the narrow red tie and stood just looking into the mirror. He thought of years on the coast and how he took great pride, and care, in dressing smartly before going out for the evening. He went to take his position at the entrance and noticed several new persons present to help on this special evening. Wadus stared at a bartender, whose back was to him, as he readied his bar in the rear of the great room. He walked slowly until he stood close behind the bartender and said, "How about a black velvet, club soda, and a slice of lime."

The tall, thin, bartender spun around quickly as if having been suddenly awakened and shouted as he hurried from behind the counter and threw both arms around Wadus."WADUS! Wadus, how th hell are you man? I've asked about you a hundred times and nobody on the coast has seen you, or knows anything. Man, what th hell are you doing here? I heard some bad shit. Rumor has it that you were in jail, those don't look like jail clothes to me. Damn, it's good to see you."

"Thanks Deano, it's great to see you too, I couldn't believe it was you when I glanced back here. Aren't you still bartending in Myrtle Beach?

"Yeah, I'm still there. A friend of mine asked me to come up and fill in for him here cause he had something else to do at the last minute."

"Well, maybe all of these high rollers will make it worth your while with some extra good tips."

"Tips! Tips from this bunch! Hell no man. They'll go to a thousand dollar a plate political dinner, which they write off their taxes, but they wouldn't give a working man spit. If the truth were known most of them probably own businesses and bitch about paying their help a minimum wage. No Wadus, I'd rather be at a working man's bar. I'd do much better as far as the money is concerned. I just did this as a favor to my buddy.

132

Tell me about yourself. Why haven't you been down? Everybody really wonders about you."

"Deano, please don't say anything about seeing me. I'm in Central Prison and have a lot of years to serve. I work here at the mansion on a work detail."

"Damn, Wadus, I did hear about the accident, but I didn't think you'd get much time for what you did. You should have killed the bastards."

"Deano, it's great to see you, and I'll be talking with you some more before the night's over but I've got to run."

"Right. Go Heels," as he watched Wadus leave the room.

Wadus made one final check upstairs to make sure everything was as it should be. As he passed the Governor's bedroom Mrs. Trout called, "Wadus, come in here a minute."

"Yes ma'am," as he entered the bedroom where she stood in just a short silk slip. He turned around quickly and said, "Excuse me ma'am I—."

"Oh don't be such a prude. Come over here I need your male opinion."

Wadus cautiously walked over as she pointed to two long dresses on the bed she asked, "Which one, I can't decide, you choose."

Wadus tried to focus all of his attention on the two gowns and replied, "They are both lovely ma'am."

"Which one Wadus?"

"The black one ma'am."

She picked the black dress up, put it over her head, slithered and wiggled it down her body. She turned in several directions in front of the mirror and asked, "Why is this one your choice?"

"I think it enhances your beautiful blond hair and fair skin."

"Really, you think so?"

"Yes ma'am."

She backed up close to Wadus and said, "Well, zip me up Wadus." He did so and she turned to face him and asked, "What other suggestions, and be honest and frank." Wadus hesitated and she said, "Come on Wadus."

He reluctantly answered, "In my opinion you should lose some of your jewelry."

"Really, this is all expensive and beautiful jewelry."

"Yes ma'am too much so; it diminishes your natural beauty."

"Go on Wadus."

"Ma'am you have fine long arms, fingers, and hands. The diamond and wedding band accentuate their beauty, but the rest detracts from it. Like the Greeks said, "Beauty without extravagance."

Mrs. Trout took off bracelets and several rings and stared at Wadus who said, "Yes indeed ma'am, you are more beautiful, but it's only my opinion."

She came closer until she was almost touching him and looked silently into his face and said, "Well, don't I appeal to you?"

"Please, if there's nothing more ma'am I have to get down stairs."

"Well, if that's what you must do." Wadus left the room quickly and hurried to take his position at the entrance of the mansion.

Ms. Clark arrived first and was greeted by her appointed doorman. Wadus said nothing. He did not have the words as he studied her stunning beauty from head to toe. Such beauty was best just beheld in silence. Her reaction was much the same as she gazed at inmate 204 and slowly walked around him. In her low sensual voice she said, "My God Wadus I knew you would be handsome but never expected this. You give new meaning to masculine sex appeal." She leaned over close and inhaled, "You have some of the cologne on. You be careful. I may have gone too far."

"What do you mean?"

"I know the females who will be here tonight. They are not exactly the shy types. Don't make me jealous now." She left to make last minute inspections as the guests began to arrive. Mrs. Trout soon came down the stairs. She was beautiful and her only jewelry was the wedding rings and a nice necklace.

Most of the guests arrived, and then Wadus went to serve drinks. He moved about the large room taking requests for drinks mostly from females. Ms. Clark was right. They were not shy. He was visually appraised, whispered about, and by the end of the cocktail hour had been handed four cards with ladies' names and telephone numbers. As everyone made his way toward the dinning room several ladies were talking with Mrs. Trout and were most interested in knowing more about her waiter and butler. Mrs. Trout finally answered them all by saying, "I'm sorry ladies, but he has already been spoken for."

One lady inquired, "Oh really, by whom?"

"The state. He's an inmate from Central Prison. In fact I believe he'll be occupied for the next twenty years or so."

There was a gasp from the ladies and one said, "What a pity. His presence is so intense, and knowing he's an inmate makes him even more fascinating."

Wadus was not needed and avoided having to serve during the dinner hour. He took his place in the ballroom as the band began to play and the guests drifted in slowly. He moved about once again, taking orders, and fetching cocktails.

Wadus had just delivered a tray of drinks as he turned to face a smiling Debra Trout. She took the tray, placed it on a table, and taking his right hand began pulling him toward the dance floor.

"No, No, Honey, I can't do that! I'm not allowed."

It was too late, he was on the dance floor, and the band began to play the song Debra had requested. It was, "I'm a Girl Watcher" by the Okaysions. The first tune she had seen Wadus shag to which had thrilled her so much. Wadus had no option and taking Debra's hand established a rhythmic movement to the tune, looked at her and said, "O.K. Honey, show'em what you've learned, let's burn'em down." She had learned well and was able to match his steps and movements. He twirled her arm over her head, doing the male and female turns keeping in step with each other as the band added extra effort and bounce to the number. The entire group focused upon their performance and was surprised and delighted that the Governor's daughter was so good at a dance many remembered from more carefree years. Everyone applauded loudly as the music ended and Debra threw her arms around his neck and said, "Oh, thank you Wadus, thank you."

A lady leaned over and whispered to another, "He's not quite the typical prisoner, how would you like to have him as a captive? I wonder if my husband could get one like him for our home?" They both laughed.

Wadus saw Ms. Clark standing to the side; she appeared to be in shock, smiled and slightly shook her head. He knew he had not heard the last of this from her by any means.

The last guests left at 1 a.m. and Wadus was glad to see his room and to be alone. It was a great relief to know the event was over, but he was sure it would not be the last.

The following weekend Mrs. Trout and Debra went home to the mountains to visit family and friends. The Governor was not able to accompany them because of a Saturday commitment. It was Saturday evening about 9:30 when the Governor tapped on the open door of Wadus's room. Wadus was lying on the bed reading. The desk lamp was the only light on and he sat up quickly as the Governor entered his quarters.

"Do you mind if I join you for a little while?"

"No sir, come right in."

The Governor held a cocktail, and as he sat down at the desk it was obvious to Wadus it was not his first that evening as he said, "Grace and Debra are away for the weekend, I hate being alone up there. You sure you don't mind me bothering you?"

"You're not bothering me sir, I know a little about loneliness myself."

As the Governor finished the last of his drink he asked, "Wadus do you drink, I mean did you drink, you know what I mean?"

"Yes sir I did."

"What did you drink?"

"I usually had a black velvet with club soda and a slice of lime."

"How did liquor affect you, I mean you weren't one of those crazies when you drank were you?"

"No sir, in fact it seemed to have an opposite effect. It usually made me more sensitive and aware of small details, and I became more observant."

"Well, my glass is empty. Do you want a drink Wadus?" This was the last question Wadus expected to be asked by the

Governor of N.C. and before he could answer the Governor ordered, "Wadus go get us a bottle of Crown Royal, a bottle of Black Velvet, water, soda, ice, and whatever we need. Go on now, hurry back."

Wadus did as he was told and soon returned. The Governor had moved from the desk and now sat on the bed with his back against the wall. Wadus fixed him another drink and sat down at the small desk as the Governor said, "Go on, fix yourself a drink."

Wadus mixed himself a drink and the first sip transported him back in time as he briefly closed his eyes to capture the picture. The Governor had several more and Wadus was on his fourth but it seemed like eight due to the time since he had last savored the taste of whiskey. They had mostly exchanged trivial comments to this point but the Governor became calmly serious and said, "Wadus, Grace told me about you helping her pick the dress for the party the other night. You know what else she told me?"

"No sir I don't."

"My wife, Grace, the woman I love, told me you could have kissed her. In fact she said she wanted you to kiss her, but you didn't. I thank you for not kissing my wife, Wadus, but why didn't you?"

Wadus looked directly, and seriously, into the Governors eyes for several moments and then said, "I didn't because I saw too many other things. I saw your wife, I saw you, your daughter, and I remembered a time several years ago when I did give in to the weakness of the flesh."

"Wadus how long have you been divorced?"

"About nine years."

"Did you have a lot of ladies before you went to prison?"

"Only one sir."

"You know, I love my wife more than ever, and I've never been unfaithful to her. I think she loves me. It's just that I don't see the sparkle and excitement in her eyes and personality that was there when we are together. I mean it seems our relationship is just a routine to her, and she doesn't really respond like she once did."

"She still loves you very much sir, she proved that by telling you about me. She has just forgotten why she loves you so much. It's like Dr. John Gray says sir, 'women are from Venus and men are from Mars,' there is much truth in what he points out. I do know this, if a man does not have a love affair with his lady, wife, girlfriend, someone else will."

"Is that what happened to your marriage?"

"Yes it probably was. To sustain a long lasting love affair it takes work, effort, planning, and always remembering no one ever really owns anyone else. Millions of both sexes forget that far too often. You love someone because of the way she makes you feel and visa versa. Each has to cause the other to desire them above all others."

"Give me another drink. Wadus I read your file. You taught psychology for some years didn't you?"

"Yes sir I did, but I probably learned more than I taught."

"Well, I've had enough to drink to listen, and you've had enough to talk. Now, talk to me. Give me some insight into this situation, some advice, give me some hope of avoiding losing my wife's love."

Wadus was now pouring his sixth drink and felt no reluctance in responding to the Governor's request. He said, "Sir you must remember all the reasons why you first fell in love with her. You must make her feel more desirable, exciting, sensual, and more beautiful than she has ever felt. You must take your time, communicate, communicate, communicate, and work from her head down. The first thing I'd do is rearrange the bedroom. Keep the music, get rid of that big T.V. and some of that unnecessary furniture. Find a small round table, buy some nice room fragrance. Get a small refrigerator for chilled wine, glasses, and whatever. A big candle is great for a little romantic light too. Make her look forward to being in that room with you. There are flowers all over this house everyday, but one rose on her pillow, purchased by you, would eclipse all the others."

The Governor was now leaning forward showing his keen interest and said, "Yes I can do all that, no problem. Now what else?"

"Libido satisfaction is next, and is very important, and is why you must work from the head down. Governor the vast majority of women, especially married women, who have sexual intercourse are never prepared properly. The man feels the urge, rolls onto her and when he's satisfied rolls off. And usually says, "Wasn't that great honey." Well, I can tell you it wasn't great for her and she probably subconsciously resents him for thinking he is satisfying her so completely. Now, you tell me, how is that guy going to compete with a man who knows the difference between making love to a woman and just having sex? He's not, done deal, she's gonso."

"I believe what you say is right, but how the hell is a man to know what to do?"

"You work at it, you think about it, explore everything and I mean everything. You communicate, you take your time, you give her time to prepare her body to receive you."

The Governor burped loudly and said, "Well go on man, give me the entire game plan, the whole play book."

"O.KKKKaay. Mister, you asked, now I'm gonna tell'ya, first let me get another B.V. and soda."

Slurring his words the Governor said, "Gooood idea, pour me one too."

Wadus slowly poured the drinks, spilled a little, steadied himself as he sat and leaned over close and stared the Governor in the face as he said, "After atmosphere and communication, then comes foreplay. Oral sex!"

The Governor jerked back his head, "ORAL SEX! Damn Wadus!"

"That's right oral sex. I know it has only one meaning to most men but oral sex means exploring the entire body, and making love, with your mouth and tongue. It doesn't mean just the genitals. If you want to go there that's cool too, but not quickly, or maybe not at all, but you still must employ oral sex. It is an art, much thought, practice, and observation goes into becoming really good at it. You gently, lightly, spider-kiss your partner's entire body. Always take your time, barely licking her neck, ears, behind her knees, her thighs, and breasts. Let her feel your hot breath blowing gently on her as you retrace your moves from feet to head, always keep your hands busy, hold her buttocks with both hands and massage, rub your cheeks slowly up and down her thighs, lick and suck her fingers. Turn her onto her stomach and continue with the back. You will learn other techniques and special spots, she loves and which excite her. And if you do go down on her make it the final move, with gentleness. By then she has probably already had an orgasm or it will not take long for her to reach one when she is entered. And that my good Governor is Venus, and she requires time and preparation in order for both to achieve the greatest amount of love and satisfaction."

The Governor looked at Wadus as if he had just heard about sex for the first time and said, "Damn Wadus. Thank you again for not kissing Grace. God Almighty man you are dangerous. At least with women. You really think women like that stuff?"

"I'm absolutely positive. Wouldn't you? You will no doubt experience the same because she will want you to know the same glorious sensations. Remember, between man and wife, there should never be any inhibitions in the bedroom. Feel complete freedom to explore, and enjoy, the one you love. She will love you for it and your worries will vanish."

The Governor sat silently for over five minutes before he again said, "Damn Wadus," as he tried to stand. Wadus was not much better off but helped the Governor to his feet. The Governor looked seriously at his watch bringing it toward his eyes and back away from them as he exclaimed, "Holy, it's 2:45 in the morning, good night." He stopped at the door and said, "Wadus, I think you better help me, I haven't been this drunk since I was in law school. Don't you tell Grace about this."

"No sir, I won't." He hooked his right arm under the Governor's left and they slowly staggered through the mansion eventually reaching the bottom of the stairway. They both hesitated and looked up at the obstacle before them. Wadus said, "Governor, you hold on to my arm now and I'm gonna hold on to this rail and maybe we can make it to the top without killing ourselves." The Governor laughed, and they began what seemed an endless journey but finally reached the top and made it to the Governor's bedroom.

Wadus helped him onto his bed and the Governor said, "Don't leave me alone, Wadus. I don't want to be alone. Sit with me for awhile."

"Yes sir." and he sat in a large chair across the room. He remembered the nights he had done the same for his son. He did not like to be alone either. He thought of how terrible, and destructive, loneliness is for those who are not familiar with it. Darkness has a way of intensifying all things feared but seldom admitted. He awoke at 7:30 a.m. and quietly made his way to his own quarters to continue much needed sleep.

Chapter 17

The Flesh Is Weak
*"The sins they do two by two
they must pay for one by one."* Kipling

The following week Ms. Clark instructed Wadus and Jefferson to make a number of changes in the Governor's bedroom. The Governor and his wife spent much more time there, and there was new spirit in their personalities. She smiled, laughed, giggled, held on to the Governor and whispered to him much, much more. The entire staff was very aware, and amused, at their unusual joy and almost adolescent exchanges of affection. Ms. Clark was happy with this refreshing new atmosphere but tried extremely hard to be analytical. She asked Wadus many questions as her keen eye had observed the Governor's increasing demands upon Wadus to come to his office and more frequent quick chats in passing. Wadus would only slightly raise his arms, look dumb, and say, "Love, who can figure such matters of the heart?"

"I sense you can figure more than you are willing to admit Mr." She teased him often about his dancing performance. "Just when I think I know all about you, you blow my mind by showing me dancing like I've never seen before. And by the way, I was very jealous, and I'm not going to inflate your ego by repeating some of the female reactions to your presence, not to mention the shagging. You're really going to answer to me big time someday. And don't ever again mention the difference in our ages. You've got moves I've never seen. Big show off, and don't think you won't have to teach me because you will."

"Trina darling, you know how I feel about you, but Baby by the time I'm out I'd have to teach you on crutches. I feel so badly that you are missing so much—."

She did not allow him to finish and walking away said, "I don't want to hear it, just be ready Mister."

Wadus was grateful to know such a beautiful creature had feelings for him but felt guilty because the reality of time signaled great disappointment for them both.

Debra entered her senior year of high school and the Governor approached the fourth year of his term. Debra was doing well and looked forward to attending UNC at Chapel Hill the following year. She was confident of being accepted. The Governor was equally as sure he would not be accepted for another term in office. He had vetoed many appropriation bills and had alienated most of the power brokers of his own party. He could count on support from only a few of the youngest representatives who had not yet been contaminated by the system. His party finally informed him they intended to run another candidate and strongly urged him to announce he would not seek a second term. It would be less embarrassing for him, his family, the party, and all concerned. He called for Wadus that evening around 9 p.m. and confided in this inmate much as one would confess to a priest.

He was more despondent than Wadus had ever seen him. "What do you intend to do sir?"

"I'm going to veto every piece of pork that comes across my desk for the next year. Then I am going to take my family and go home, where I wish I had stayed."

"The first part is good, the second is a bad idea."

"Why is it a bad idea?"

"I just hate to see a man back down from a fight when he's right. Especially you, sir. Yeah, you may be licked, but won't be destroyed. If you go back home let it be the people of N.C. who send you and not the hounds."

The Governor shook his head and said, "Do you know how much money it takes to run for office? Those hounds control that money, and besides, they're going to run someone else."

"Run anyway, run as an Independent. That's the last thing they expect you to do. Right now they are probably having cocktails, smoking cigars, and laughing about how they are running the hillbilly back to his mountains. If you announce you're running on an independent ticket their plan will backfire. The news media will begin to ask them some embarrassing questions. Furthermore, you have another year in office and will be the incumbent. You can get a tremendous amount of media coverage, campaigning, and travel by nature of your position. Also, if you sponsor, and propose legislation which will help the average working Carolinian I think you'd see a lot of small contributions start coming in. The people are out-there, Governor. They need you, you help them and they'll help you. Just don't run from that bunch."

"That was quite a pep talk, and I would like to get a few licks in, but I am a realist. Besides, I haven't even told Grace anything about this situation, and deep down I think she'll be glad to go back home."

"Yes sir that is an important factor. Good night Governor." He went to his room and hoped this good man would find peace, and closure, regardless of his decision to go or to stay.

Wadus continued his daily routine and grew increasingly fond of his friends in the kitchen and of the Governor's family. Everyone, except himself, seemed to have forgotten he was an inmate. He reminded himself often and tried to remain as silent and observant as possible. He called his friend Mohamet occasionally and when possible would ask to spend the weekend at Central in cell 101. The first time he asked the Governor for permission to do so the Governor was shocked.

"Wadus, I have to be very frank, just what is your relationship with this inmate at Central? Are you gay? Please be honest, I won't hold it against you if you are."

"No sir, indeed not, neither is he. In fact he saved me from being raped and protected me all the time I was in Central. He's a Muslim, a black man who never really had a chance. I helped him learn to read, and to teach himself, he protected me from the prison perversion. We became very close friends. I hope he will someday be free, and I like to contact and encourage him to work toward that end. No sir, I'm not gay, my libido is probably too strong for a man my age."

144

"I understand. Wadus, I listen to you say you hope this man will be paroled and free eventually, but I've never heard a single word from you about your own sentence nor have I seen any desire from you for your freedom. In fact, most of the time I forget your are an inmate. What would you do, or like to do, if you were a free man?"

Wadus shook his head slowly and said, "Sir, I'm not really sure now. For a very long time all I could think of was going to find my son."

"Find your son. Wadus, I thought your son had died?"

"Yes sir, he did, but I know he's somewhere and maybe that's where I really want to be."

"Are you telling me you're suicidal?"

"No I am not. I don't have the courage, or whatever it takes to do that. I'm just saying that for a long, long time freedom was of little matter to me."

The Governor granted his permission and Wadus was allowed to visit Mohamet from time to time.

The Governor's questions often haunted Wadus as he lay in the dark and reflected upon the answers he had given. His conscience bothered him as he realized he was slowly developing a desire to live. He felt somewhat guilty. He reasoned it to be the result of Ms. Clark's interest in him, her beauty, his weaknesses, and he prayed never to be the cause of her waiting only to be disappointed. He thought of the Governor's question of why he had not kissed his wife, and if he were gay. These thoughts took him back in time to his last, and only intimate, relationship since his divorce.

He had been divorced almost five years and spent much time on the coast. She was very attractive, for her age, and he had immediately noticed her the first time she entered the lounge where he was having a cocktail. Yes, he thought, how attractive, but she is not wearing the cosmetic of happiness. He sensed something troubling, yet interesting, in this unknown female. As was his custom he made notes in his daily logbook of his observations and curiosities. Eventually, after seeing her on several separate evenings, she walked over and asked if she could sit with him. He had replied he would enjoy the company. It was the beginning of months of encounters, and conversations, between them in this tavern. He continued to listen, observe carefully, and to record information as if preparing a psychological profile as he had done many times in counseling. They both enjoyed communicating, and over the months she revealed her deepest secrets, and feelings, to him. She was, and had been, married for many years. She did not love her husband and admitted to having had affairs. He recorded it all and slowly began to see a troubled personality form on paper. He never revealed this clandestine study to her nor made any attempt to distance himself from this troubled female. After almost a year they became intimate on a rainy evening when he had had far too many cocktails. He had not only ignored his psychological research, but also his principles and had surrendered to the weakness of the flesh. He had committed the same sin that had been committed against him. She left her husband and was soon spending many nights at Wadus's cottage professing extreme joy, love, and satisfaction. He continued his documented, but secret, profile study and discovered more than he ever expected or wanted to know. He hated himself for having done this profile and for not revealing it to her. He agonized for there was nothing he could do to reverse the personality disorders that had developed over many years. He knew what she would do, was doing, and why. He withdrew for weeks at a time yet returned to watch her play out her destiny and deceit.

She was a functioning schizophrenic. This had led to numerous personality- disorders over the years. Her two personalities competed for dominance and eventually the destructive one emerged victorious. The good personality hid but would someday return with a vengeance.

She could not help being what she was and he only felt deep sorrow for her for no one ever escapes time and truth. Loneliness, depression, and tears would ultimately be her final companions.

He prayed for her, wherever she was, and for forgiveness of his weaknesses of the flesh.

Chapter 18

A Trip To The Future
*"There was a wise man in the East
whose constant prayer was that he
might see today with the eyes of tomorrow."*
Alfred Mercier

Ms. Clark waited for the right private moment and found Wadus cleaning in the Governor's office. It was early October and had been only a few days since he had encouraged the Governor to seek re-election. He had no way of knowing what had transpired between the governor and Mrs. Trout and was deep in thought of these matters when Ms. Clark spoke, "Wadus, I'm glad I found you alone. I have something I need to tell you."

"I was thinking of something and I didn't hear you come in, what is it?"

"It isn't really a major event, but I wanted you to know I will be away for a week. They are insisting I use some of the many weeks I've accumulated so I'm going on a little vacation. I'll miss you and I wanted you to know why I wasn't here. Guess where I'm going?"

"Paris, Rome, Vienna, probably someplace very exciting, I hope so anyway."

"You and I will go to those places later. No, I'm going down to the coast. I want to walk on Sunset Beach, see Little River, and some of the places you've told me of in North Myrtle Beach. I've often dreamed of what you call your little kingdom by the sea, and now I'm really excited about getting an actual picture of what I've imagined it to be. No, I've been to Rome; I want to go where I know you long to be and see where I hope to be with you someday."

Wadus looked into her beautiful, excited eyes, walked over closed the door and locked it. She stood as if she were in her bridal nightgown expecting to finally know her man intimately. He walked slowly over and put his hands softly on her face and silently admired what he had never dreamed of experiencing again. She breathed deeply as he gently touched her cheeks with his finger- tips. He then put both arms around her and drew her to his body. He ran his hand through her radiant long hair and in almost a whisper spoke into her ear, "Trina darling, I love you so much and I'm not capable of telling, or showing, you how much. Please know and always remember this. Now listen to me darling. Don't do this. Don't dream your beautiful life away hoping for a miracle, an impossible miracle. Go someplace and meet young men who are good men and able to give you the wonderful life you deserve. A prisoner, inmate 204, is holding you right now and occasionally this is all it will ever be. Please listen to me and think about the truth of what you hear. I can survive as inmate 204, but I cannot live thinking I am responsible for you being a prisoner and doing my time. If you go down there it will only make us both miserable knowing we cannot likely ever be there together."

She pulled back, and with tears in her eyes said, "Dream of mine, it may be just a dream, but for me it is a dream of ecstasy. I am a dreamer by nature, and if I cannot have what I want I do not want anything. Now, you feel guilty if you like, but it isn't going to change anything. Don't ever talk about being a prisoner again. You shouldn't be anyway, and I don't ever think of you as one. I have to believe we will awake and find it wasn't just a dream. I am going to the coast."

"God I love, and admire, your stubborn unrealistic commitment. You are the epitome of what a man hopes to find as a lover and soul mate. Very few ever do."

"That's right so don't try to avoid the small amount of happiness we are able to trap. I certainly don't intend to."

Wadus hesitated for a moment, looked at her and said, "O.K., if you're determined to go there I want you to do it right. Do you have reservations yet?"

"No, I'll just wait and pick out a nice place around North Myrtle Beach. This time of year there shouldn't be any problem finding one."

"No, don't do that. I want you to stay at my place. There isn't a telephone, or television, but everything else is right there and ready."

"Wadus, that's wonderful. I had intended to try to find it anyway, you know, just to see what the outside looked like. I'll clean it up for you. I imagine it needs a good cleaning since you've been away so long."

"No, Baby, you will not need to do anything, everything is cleaned, and washed, weekly."

She was surprised to hear this and wondered how he could arrange such matters from the isolation he had lived for the past several years.

Wadus stepped over to the desk, took a pen and small piece of paper and wrote a number on it. He handed it to her saying, "Don't lose this. When you arrive call this number and ask to speak to J.J. When you get him just say, "J.J., Wadus said to call you," he'll tell you exactly what to do. That's all you need say, now don't forget it Baby. No one has used that number since I've been here."

"I don't understand how you could—."

"Sweetheart, you'll know everything all in due time. We used to say it's a poor dog that doesn't bury a bone." He told her of many places to stop and gave her several names to inquire about then said, "Baby be careful down there, don't be afraid, but be careful. Be sure to take some long walks at Sunset Beach. It will be cool, but sunny, and there will be only a few people. Now lastly, please don't use my name very much, only with J.J. and a few others, the less they know about my life now, the better."

Trina Clark left the following morning to enjoy a week of well- deserved vacation. It was a lovely autumn day, and she enjoyed being away from the city as she drove south. She followed Rt. 40 to Wilmington and Rt. 17 south and stopped in

Calabash. It was 12:45 when she dialed the number Wadus had given her. A man answered and she inquired, "Is this J.J.?"

"Yes."

"Wadus told me to call you."

"Wadus! Yes, good, where are you?" She told him where she was in Calabash and described the car she was driving and he said, "You wait right there and I'll be there in fifteen minutes." It was less time than she expected when a pick up truck pulled beside her car. A middle-aged black man walked to her window and said, "Ma'am, I'm J.J." She introduced herself and was told to follow his truck. She followed for several miles before he turned off taking a side road for another short distance and slowly pulled into a driveway. He waited for her to get out and stretching his arm toward the house said, "This is Wadus's place. Come on I let you in and show you where everything is." J.J. unlocked the door and Trina Clark's heart pounded with anticipation. He took her upstairs, then showed her the downstairs. He finally said, "Ms. Clark, I know you must be a special person cause you are the first Wadus has allowed in here for years. That is, except me, and my wife. We come and give it a good cleaning every week. The telephone and T.V. are not hooked up but everything else is just like he left it. Ms. Clark, I get money every month from some office in Raleigh, but I don't hear nothing from or about Wadus. How is he doing?"

Trina knew there was sincere concern and a special friendship between the man and Wadus. She replied, "Wadus is healthy and, you know where he is in Raleigh, so considering that, I suppose it's the best that can be hoped for at this time. I hope that someday he will be able to return here because he loves this place so much. I can see why."

"Ms. Clark, you probably have one of those cell phones so if you need anything, day or night, just call and I'll be right over. I have another key so whenever you leave just put that one on the coffee table and lock the door from the inside."

Trina Clark made several attempts to gather more information about Wadus from this man, but he would only reveal they were close friends.

J.J. left and she began to slowly explore every detail of the house. She loved it and felt comfortable and at peace. She took her bags to the larger of two upstairs bedrooms as she reasoned it was where Wadus slept. Putting her suitcase down she said, "Wadus, if I can't sleep with you, at least tonight I'll sleep in your bed, and pretend you're beside me." She sat and gazed about the room and suddenly it struck her. The room reeked of sensuality and seduction. There was a small circular teakwood table, a large scented candle in the center, and two cozy chairs. There was a very small refrigerator in the corner, a wine rack, a small stereo, and the fragrance of applejack in the air. She felt hurt, and jealous, as she thought another woman had probably shared this room with the man she so dearly loved. She cast these feelings aside as she said out loud, "That was B.T., 'Before Trina', there won't be any A.T.'s, 'After Trina,' I guarantee you Mr. Wadus." She also thought, it isn't as large but this arrangement reminds me of the changes I made in the Governor's bedroom. She shook her head, laughed, and said, "Wadus Strickland you rascal, no wonder Mrs. Trout acts like a new woman." She felt good knowing Wadus was so sensual yet shy, honest, and keenly aware of the needs of a female. She left the house and walked around the outside. There were many beautiful trees, large pines, oaks, dogwoods, and a huge magnolia tree. Birds of many varieties were feeding from the large sunflower feeders, and she thought of how he had even provided for them in his absence. She spent considerable time outside and returned to explore more of the inside. She opened closets where many fine suits, shirts, ties and pairs of dressy shoes were stored. She knew he was a man who dressed extremely well. She wanted to take a nap on his bed but the urge to walk on Sunset Beach was almost an assignment. She drove only a few minutes and was there. It was late afternoon, sunny, and chilly with a pleasant wind from the ocean. The beach was beautiful, and she walked a great distance listening to the surf as it repeatedly kissed the beach reminding her of Wadus and his low, gentle, and peaceful voice. She now understood why he the thought of his small cottage and this magnificent beach as his little kingdom by the sea. She thought, if he were only here, we would never return to Raleigh.

She returned to the cottage, showered, dressed and went to Calabash for a seafood dinner for which this small fishing village was famous. She ate at The Calabash Seafood House Wadus had recommended. She was unable to eat all of the large portions served and left much on the plate. Upon presenting her ticket the cashier asked "Ma'am you left a lot of food, was anything wrong?"

"No indeed not, it was delicious. There was just so much I couldn't eat it all. As the cashier took the ticket and money Ms. Clark said, "Yes, a man named Wadus told me to eat here, he said the food was excellent."

The cashier stopped, looked intently at her and asked, "Do you know Wadus Strickland?"

"Yes, quite well."

The cashier handed her money back, tore the ticket in half and said, "Your dinner is on Calabash Seafood House, and you tell Wadus we're mad at him for not staying in touch, but we still love him anyway."

"Thank you so much, and I certainly will tell him. Good night and thank you again."

She returned to the cottage as the exhaustion, excitement, and peacefulness of the day was rapidly calling her to sleep. Before going upstairs she checked the refrigerator and found a bottle of cold white zenfandel and a frosty wineglass. She poured a glass and went to the bedroom. A gentle rain had begun to fall outside as she inspected the collection of C.D.s. She put "Unchained Melody" in the stereo, lit the candle on the small table and turned off the lights. She sat beside the table, sipped the wine, smelled the apple cinnamon candle, and listened to the beautiful song, rain, and thought of the years she had dreamed of such a scene. Wadus was the only missing element, but she felt his presence as if he were in the chair across the small table. Finishing the wine, and turning off the stereo, she began to get ready for bed. She stood in the candle light and slowly took off everything until completely naked and looked at herself in the mirror as she said, "Dream of mine, I'll never sleep in your bed with anything on, ever." She turned back the sheets and fell into a secure dream world of beauty and complete contentment.

The following day she spent much time, and thought, taking long walks on the beach. During the days that followed she prepared several meals at the cottage and ate out a number of times. She visited several dance clubs Wadus had mentioned such as Fat Harold's. He had told her, "If you see a small bartender about my age with a bar cloth with each end tucked into his back pockets, tell him I said Hello. His name is Marcus." She visited this club which was crowded with many middle age men and women enjoying shagging to the oldies beach music. She quickly recognized the bar tender, with the bar cloth in both back pockets, and ordered a drink. When he served it she said, "Are you Marcus?"

"Yes I am."

"Wadus said to say Hello for him."

Marcus's reaction was much the same as the cashier's in the restaurant as he stopped, stared, and asked, "Is Wadus alright?"

"Yes, considering."

"You tell him I said to take care of himself and get back down here as soon as possible. I made a trip up there, but he was out on some work detail and I didn't get to see him. Are you his lady?"

"Yes, I mean I like to think so anyway."

"Good, your drinks are on me."

She watched the shagging, had two drinks, and was hit-on at least a dozen times. Two were persistent and quite aggressive. Marcus was quickly there saying, "Hey guy, don't bother this lady, she's with me. Take it on down the line, O.K." They moved away post-haste as Marcus said, "Some of these guys don't know when to take no for an answer and move on."

Wadus was right to say "be careful." She finished her drink and looked forward to a glass of wine upstairs in the cottage before bed.

She had a wonderful week and felt sad about leaving but looked forward to seeing Wadus. It seemed much longer than a week since she had talked with him. Before leaving she called J.J and tried to give him some money, but he said, "No ma'am, absolutely not. Miss Trina, tell Wadus he don't have to send me money, and I've got all that's been sent right here when he needs it. Tell 'em to come home soon as he can."

"Yes I will, J.J., and I know Wadus will appreciate it. Thank you for everything and I hope to see you again."

153

As she drove back to Raleigh her thoughts were on Wadus Strickland. What was it about this unobtrusive, quiet, man that reached out and touched others like a feather making them feel he knew them well? Why did this man, a prisoner in Central Prison, have the loyalty and respect of so many from the capitol to the coast? She did not know why, only that he was unusual, mysterious, and very special. She thought how she had loved him one week earlier and how much more she loved him now. She silently said, "Please God, grant my prayer."

The following morning Ms. Clark found Wadus in the kitchen and asked, "Wadus, would you please clean my office? I don't think it has been touched since I left?"

"Yes ma'am." He knew it did not need cleaning for he had cleaned it on Friday.

Shawna snapped, "Just when I start liking that white woman she gets that attitude and all bossieafied. Do this, do that."

"Hush gal, ten ta yo own job, youngun yo don't know nothin."

Wadus gathered his cleaning materials and went to Ms. Clark's office. As he entered she walked to the door and closed it behind him, turned and said, "Honey, the office is fine. I just wanted you in here." She walked over, put her arms around his neck, and kissed him passionately. She then said, "Thank you, Wadus, I love your place. I didn't want to leave." She talked quickly, and enthusiastically, as she told him all about her week. He listened and enjoyed her excitement and the sparkling dance in her beautiful eyes. She said, "Now Mister, about that bedroom of yours. I have one question. Did you have a lot of women there?"

"I suppose you mean after I was divorced."

"Yes."

"Only one. She was a mistake, my fault, a weakness of the flesh."

"I knew you would be honest, and I can't help feeling jealous. Just understand I was the last woman who slept in your bed, and I intend to be the next and final one. Do you understand? No Wadus, seriously, I'm so afraid you won't love me and want me."

Wadus reached and gently placed his hand on her cheek and said, "Trina darling, if I live to walk out of Central a free man, I promise you if you are not there, there will never be a woman there. I only regret seeing you wait for something so important which may never happen. I feel so guilty."

She kissed him again and said, "I love loving you. Don't ever feel guilty for giving me what I feel, even if I never have anything else."

Chapter 19

Crossing The Rubicon
*"No great advance has ever been made
in science, politics, or religion, without controversy."*
Lyman Beecher

Governor Trout's third year in office had ended. He had alienated the most powerful men in the N.C. legislature and it was assumed by all he would not seek a second term in office.

Wadus was called to his office in the mansion late that evening and it had been several weeks since his discussion with the Governor. He expected to be asked to fetch something the Governor wanted and was not prepared for what followed. He entered the office, "Yes sir, would you like something?"

"Wadus, close the door and sit down." He did as told and the Governor continued, "Grace and I have talked much about the present situation and have considered all the points you made when we last talked. She wants to go home to the mountains, but she's a scrapper and she's furious. She agrees with you, we may indeed go home next year, but it should be the people of N.C. who decide and not that bunch of mammonites in the legislature. Now, this is the most unorthodox union in the history of politics, and we may be wrong, however we have decided you will be the unknown secret captain of this campaign. Your ideas are so radical, but right, at least this hillbilly will be heard from. I will expect you to devote most of your time, from this point on, to presenting me with ideas. I want you to be critically objective in pointing out the pros and cons on every small detail. No one, absolutely no one, is to ever know you exist or that you have any involvement with me other than serving coffee. Is this clear and do you agree?"

Wadus was silent, and serious, for several moments and replied, "Yes sir, I understand and agree, I would not have it any other way. But sir, there is one thing I feel you should consider at this point. It maybe far fetched, but at least consider it."

"What is that?"

"Governor, how well do you remember your Roman History?"

"What's that got to do with anything?"

"Maybe nothing, maybe a great deal. Everyone knows the fate of Julius Caesar, but not many have considered the "why" and what underlying message there is for all generations of political leaders. Caesar wasn't killed in a robbery, a bar, by a run away chariot, or a mob. He was murdered in the Roman Senate, by the most educated and sophisticated lawmakers in the world. How could such brilliant men commit such a dastardly deed? The answer sir is money and power. Oh, they told the common people Caesar wanted to end the Republic and wanted to be a dictator. The truth is the Republic had already ended and in reality Caesar had dictatorial powers. The main point, and reason, Caesar was murdered was because of the reforms he had made. Within two years he had limited the amount of land the wealthy could own, started a massive public works program putting thousands of unemployed to work, he streamlined the bureaucracy eliminating tremendous financial wastes, made changes in the calendar, and finally he went too far. He revised the tax code and forced the wealthy patrician class to pay their fair share. These were the people who murdered Caesar and these were the reasons why. Sir, people who have great wealth and power do not like changes which threaten their positions and privileges. Be it ancient Rome or present North Carolina. The more things change the more they stay the same. Sir, I just want you to consider there is danger, in varying degrees, in what you are undertaking. You are up against some real heavy hitters who play for huge stakes. They will expose your every minor flaw, error, weakness, your past all the way back to kindergarten. Then, they will go after your wife, daughter, and circulate many falsehoods about all of you. No sir, the captains and kings don't abdicate, they must be overthrown, and this can be a very dangerous goal. It will not be a walk in the park sir."

"Yes, what you say is very true, but the greater the goal, the greater the risk."

"Just at least consider the fate of Caesar. Now, have you thought about major goals to stress during your campaign?"

"I want to be the Governor remembered for making changes which help the majority of working, low and middle income, Carolinians. Ones like my parents who worked so hard, and sacrificed so much for so long, so I might receive a better education and have a better life than they had. I want your help in establishing these goals. Devote much of your time in the next two months to that end. By the time of the State of the State message I want to be ready to blow their bloomers up. Wadus, remember this must be completely secret and confidential. Within the next week we will begin meeting nightly between 9 and 10 o'clock. By that hour the staff and mansion employees have left. Concentrate upon ideas and programs that will be beneficial and receptive to the average working class majority. Keep in mind also this will be a very low budget campaign, there won't be any thousand dollar a plate dinners to raise funds."

"Yes sir, I'll start right away. I have been in prison for over three years but can't imagine the working man's status and standard of living have changed radically in such a short time."

The Governor stood up, put his hands on his hips, and said, "I am almost certain I'll be defeated soundly, but I have a good feeling about losing this way."

"I'm glad you made this decision Governor. Good night." He left the Governor and went to his quarters.

Wadus sat in the dim light of his small room in this large mansion but could not think of politics. His head ached, his mind raced, images flashed, and pimples ran the coarse of his arms as he remembered the events that had taken place since that dreadful June afternoon in 1988. How was this possible? He was an obscure man when free, now as inmate 204, asked to be an advisor, critic, and aid to the most important man in the State of North Carolina. How could this man put such trust, and faith, in him? Many hows and whys tore at his frightened mind. He did not understand any of it and was truly afraid for the second time since the death of his son. He feared the unseen power that had ordained such events in his life. He feared his ability was so much less than others perceived in him. He was only an average man who had grown accustomed to adversity, and hardship, over his entire life. He had come to consider them loyal companions often feeling uneasy when they were not present. He thought of Joseph in the Bible and tried to believe the same God was now present and still in control. He wept as he thought of Trina and how he longed to just hold her. She was not there. Tears drifted down his face as he lowered his head into his hands and prayed.

The daily schedule was much the same for inmate 204. His chores were not as time consuming as in the past and he was able to go to his room occasionally to write down some point, or thought, he wanted to explore later.

Debra Trout was a senior in high school now and doing well in her studies. She still, however, insisted Wadus be present after school. He would mostly just look over what she was doing in history class and then just listen. She knew she could explain, and reveal, her most private adolescent thoughts to this man and be secure from criticism as well as exposure. She went through several "crushes" and was heart broken briefly after each. Wadus listened, sympathized, and gently counseled her as he hoped he would have done if she were his own child. Debra often had a friend, or several, practice shagging with her after school. Wadus was now only needed to applaud, encourage, and occasionally introduce a new move for them to master. He enjoyed this passive participation remembering the great times he had loved the same as a teenager. Ironically the dance, music, and songs were the same.

His late evenings were becoming very different as he spent most of them in the Governor's office. Many nights he was alone, making notes, and writing down possible objectives. After two weeks the Governor decided it was time to put his captive advisor to the test.

"Well Wadus, let me see, or hear, what you've come up with. Don't worry, we will probably have many disagreements before we reach a consensus."

"Yes, sir, I understand and have tried to think in terms of your primary objective. That being to be known as the common working man's Governor and friend. In order to achieve this we must get inside that man, or woman's, head. We must appreciate and understand their daily lives, schedules, hopes, fears, and mostly needs. I honestly believe the average person not only in this state but across the nation instinctively feels forgotten, used, and abused by the state and federal government. They have coped with much political, social, and economic inequity. I further believe it is the economic inequity that they resent the most and is increasingly more difficult for them to sustain. Sir, I think we need to propose radical new legislation that would so shock the masses in such a way that you would quickly get their attention. After all, we really don't have much time, and as you pointed out, money."

"Do you really think such radical objectives would have a prayer of passing through the legislature and becoming law? Hell Wadus, they would never even be introduced."

"I have considered that fact sir. You will have to be ready to play hard ball, down and dirty sir. Like Cool Hand Luke said, 'Sometimes nothing is a good hand to hold.' You have nothing to lose and everything to gain. The N.C. State Constitution has three great democratic pillars. They are initiative, referendum, and recall. They are never used. Most people don't know they exist, or what they mean. Legislators do not fear them because they have no fear of them being used. When you introduce your program you must educate the average Carolinian as to what these three principles are. You must promise you will use them if the legislature refuses to listen to the voice of the majority of North Carolinians. The majority elects these representatives, yet these representatives most often refuse to give that majority what they want and seem to think they are there to vote for only the legislation they agree with. They really shouldn't have that right. They should work for what the majority wants whether they agree with it or not. You must have a plan, a system set up and ready to go into action and prove to the people you are what you say you are.

If not, they will not believe you, and I am certain you will fail. Think like they think sir. Be one of them, be willing to wound sensitive social and political tissue. You must be willing to intimidate certain factions as they have attempted to intimidate you. Be Machiavellian for the good of the majority. Can you imagine the audacity of a legislator, such as the Speaker of the House, who says to the majority, 'I don't care what you want, "I" am not even going to allow it to come before this lawmaking body.' Does that sound like democracy to you sir?"

"Damn Wadus, you really mean to go to war don't you."

"Sir, I learned growing up in Robeson County, many years ago, when you are in a fight and don't go all the way hard and fast you are certain to lose. You may even get whipped anyway, but at least you put all you had into it. Another thing, if you do have to hurt someone, you must hurt them so badly they will never be a threat to you again. If you play a sophisticated game with these hounds they will bury you. In Central I learned you are only safe if others fear you. My cellmate proved this to me. And the fear others had of him protected me. If you do not intend to fight hard, and long, don't fight at all. Go home."

Governor Trout sat in deep thought for a considerable time and then said, "Well, speaking of Caesar, I suppose I've crossed the Rubicon so let's go for it all. I have some reservations about what can be done to gain the support of the working man, and I'm curious to hear what you think."

"You must put a few more dollars into their pockets, or at least take fewer out of those pockets. For instance, what would an hourly wage earner think about a law that would not tax labor over forty hours per week? Many will not work any overtime because they benefit very little from it and in some cases are hurt financially.

"I don't think the state could afford the loss of that tax revenue."

"On the contrary, sir, it would generate more revenue. The people would not invest these few extra dollars in stocks and bonds, they would buy consumer goods and services. This would create many jobs and more taxable forty- hour weeks. Secondly, the sales tax is so regressive and is a tremendous burden to the masses of low-income families. Do away with sales tax, especially on food and clothing, for the family earning less than thirty five thousand dollars a year. Increase sales taxes on expensive luxury items and second homes. Do away with as many tax loopholes for the wealthy as possible. This is a major grievance of the working class. Next, deal with education. At present N.C. has one of the finest university systems in the nation, yet many N.C. students are unable to attend, either because of low SAT scores or lack of funds. The public school system, at present, ranks in the lowest five percent in the nation. It must make a great leap forward and this will take much revenue as well as change. A state lottery is the answer."

"The legislature will not even consider putting it on the agenda for discussion let alone for a vote. Besides the religious right wing would destroy us if we proposed a lottery."

"That's possible, but polls indicate the majority of North Carolinians would vote yes to a lottery. Furthermore this religious right wing probably gambles on the stock market each day, and many churches sponsor raffles to raise money. Isn't that gambling? Nevertheless, it might well be the first issue to put to the people in a referendum. Let the majority say yes or no and not a despotic legislator who treats the citizens as irresponsible children and thinks he has the right to speak for millions. Sir, no one is that wise, nor is that democracy. He should be recalled by the majority and then he may come to understand that principle."

"I have over two months before the State of the State message and that is the time to announce I will be running for Governor again and all of the proposals we decide upon. Everyone, including Jacobs, assumes I will not run and will quietly fade away. Hell, they may even start the recall process on me."

"I wish there were someway, something, we could use to neutralize him. In fact it would be good if I could access a personal profile on as many of the legislators as possible. I would also like a print out of the people who contribute large amounts of money to their campaign funds and as much background on them as possible. We might discover some interesting, and possibly, useful information."

Governor Trout remembered his conversation with Warden White concerning Jacobs and said, "I know quite a lot about Jacobs, his friends, funds, but there may be something else I can use if I have to."

Governor Trout and Wadus spent many evenings during the next two months preparing, and planning, for the Governor's speech. The Governor was visited twice by Senator Jacobs. He tried to determine for sure that the Governor would not attempt to seek another term. Each time Wadus was there and he received many curious glares from the Senator. On the Senator's last visit, as Wadus served him coffee, he asked, "What did you say your name was, I remember it was an unusual one?"

"Wadus Strickland, sir."

The Senator's face indicated a purpose for asking and two days later Warden White received a call from Sentor Jacobs.

"Good afternoon Warden. This is Senator Jacobs. How are you?"

"Very good sir, what can I do for you?"

"Warden I've been in the Governor's mansion on numerous occasions and have learned the inmate assigned there is Wadus Strickland. Warden this is the man I called you about over three years ago. I explained what he had been convicted of, how the victims and their families felt, and you assured me he would do unusually hard time at Central. I'm disappointed you did not keep your word. I want him back in Central immediately and with few privileges. Now Warden, I will be very grateful, or extremely disappointed. If I am disappointed I assure you it will not be pleasant for you in the future. You have a very good position and there are others who would like to have it. Do you understand me Warden?"

"Yes, you've made yourself quite clear. Now, let me make myself as clear to you Senator. You will do nothing, unless I ask you for something, which you will then do immediately. The Governor is aware of your interest in this inmate and your attempts to use this institution to further your political goals. I am the Warden of Central Prison, and if I ever have any reason whatsoever to believe you are the cause of any problem for me, or this prison, I will immediately have several reporters from the News and Observer in my office. Lastly Senator, I don't like to use this type of vocabulary but fuck you, and if you have any friends fuck them too! Have a good day Senator."

All planning, discussion, and preparation for the State of the State speech was done in the Governor's mansion office in order to assure complete confidentially and avoid the possibility of even the slightest leak. The Governor, his wife, and Wadus were the only persons aware of the coming shock. The day arrived all too soon. The Governor and Wadus spent most of that day in the mansion office going over the speech. It became very clear to Ms. Clark, and other staff members, inmate 204 was much closer and more valued by the Governor than they had ever imagined.

Ms. Clark approached Wadus late in the afternoon and asked, "Hey fella, you've been holding out on me. What's going on?"

"I'll explain what I can tomorrow, but just be sure to watch and listen to the Governor's speech tonight. Trina, please take notes and give me your honest, and frank, opinion of what he says."

Ms. Clark gazed into his eyes, shook her head slightly, smiled and said, "You've done it to me again. Sure, I'll watch, but my mind will probably be on you and wondering what has been going on here when everyone is gone. Wadus, you frighten me sometimes, the water around you gets deeper and deeper. Please be careful."

Wadus saw concern, and fear, in her lovely eyes and said, "Please don't worry Trina, after all, the worst they could do is put me in jail." They both laughed quietly as she gave him one of her little pinches on his arm. He returned to the Governor's office, entered without knocking, and closed the door behind him.

Chapter 20

The Trustee

"Government is a trust, and the officers of the government are trustees; and both the trust and the trustees are created for the benefit of the people."
Henry Clay—Speech, 1829

Wadus waited at the front door of the mansion as the Governor, Mrs. Trout, and Debra came down the long stairway en route to the capitol building. The Governor sent Mrs. Trout and Debra on to the waiting limousine and hesitated for a word with Wadus.

"Well, inmate 204, I wish I could take you with me, but I can't so be sure to listen. I want you to know, Wadus, whatever happens from here on, good or bad, I'm glad I'm doing this."

"I know, sir, and I know you are doing the right thing. Positive, or negative, you will receive more media coverage tomorrow than in all of your first three years combined. Good luck sir." He watched as the Governor's limousine left the grounds and then hurried to his small quarters to listen to what was to follow. He listened to the applause as the Governor approached the speaker's stand in the legislature. Wadus knew only a small percentage of the people the Governor wanted to reach would be interested enough in this event to listen but hoped all would change rapidly. The Governor waited for the applause to stop, thanked them, addressed the dignitaries and began his speech.

"The State of the State of North Carolina is excellent!" There was more applause before he could continue. "Yes, it is great and strong but within the coming years it will become much greater and much stronger. It has taken me three years to learn how to be the Governor of this Great State. I apologize to the people of North Carolina for this. I am not proud of this, nor am I proud of many bills I signed into law during that learning process. I am not proud of the vast amount of the working Carolinian's money that has been spent to enhance, and further enrich, a small minority of this State's population. Yes, there are so many things I am not proud of which have come out of this capitol within the past three years. They are too numerous to list here tonight and would make little difference. I will only speak to the greatest one. The greatest resource of our Great State are the average working taxpayers and their families. Their dollars are collected, spent, and most see little value received. They are ignored, for the most part, until office seekers need their votes again in order to come here and perpetuate the status quo. This must and will change. In the coming year, and hopefully, the following four years I intend to propose legislation that will directly benefit millions of North Carolinians. Some will be expensive for upper income families, some will be extremely controversial, most of them will be radical. Radical in the sense that the will of the majority will be done, in a pure democratic and legal manner. Some, possibly many, of these programs will have to be decided by statewide referendums to truly determine the will of the majority. If necessary statewide petitions will be circulated in order to force the N.C. legislature to allow the people to decide. We must cease treating the majority of North Carolinians as adolescents who are not capable of making sound decisions."

There was very little applause by now, some mumbling, and much turning and shaking of heads.

"This often silent majority is composed of intelligent, hardworking, tax paying Carolinians who are capable of making this state a leader among all fifty states. So little has been done for the average citizen he is literally shocked when legislation is passed with his interest in mind. This should not be. Those working, paying the bills, have the right to demand the will of the majority be done. No longer can this legislature refuse to even consider issues that the people of this state want. They must be given the right to say "yes" or "no." Therefore in the coming year I shall ask this legislative body to introduce legislation that will create a statewide lottery. If defeated in the legislature I shall call for a statewide referendum to decide it once and for all. The revenue from this lottery will be used for the sole purpose of improving the quality of education in the public school system of North Carolina. Every child from Murphy to Manteo, large or small school, must receive an equal quality education. We must tremendously increase the salaries of classroom teachers in order to attract the best and most qualified persons to this vital profession. I will call for stricter, more demanding certification for this profession. I will further ask the legislature to enact a statue requiring every teacher to obtain a Masters Degree in his/her field within seven years. I will ask for statewide proficiency tests in each grade and subject before students are given credit and allowed to progress to a higher grade or be graduated. We must also provide an excellent opportunity for our young to be trained in the service industries. We must glean the best, most successful, ideas and innovations from every state. I will further ask the legislature to provide a healthy free breakfast, and lunch, for every student in the public schools of North Carolina. I will also ask for tax relief for working families spending money to educate their children beyond the high school level. No matter what it takes, regardless of what it costs, we must make a great leap forward in our educational system. The future of this Great State rests upon the shoulders of this institution. Next I call upon our lawmakers for radical changes in the tax code of North Carolina. A repeal of the sales tax on food and other essential consumer goods. I ask for an exemption of a state income tax on every hour of work over forty hours per week for the hourly wage earner. I call for a lower tax rate for workers earning less than twenty five thousand dollars per year and a much higher rate for those with incomes in excess of seventy five thousand dollars per year. We must also arrest the growth of a hungry, growing, bureaucracy. I will eliminate questionable high-paying state positions. I will veto any appropriation bill that spends needed revenue on extravagant state offices, buildings, and other facilities. I will veto any bill providing roads to golf courses, large tracts of undeveloped land or any other infrastructure which does not clearly benefit the majority of citizens in a given area. In a nutshell, I will divert millions of dollars in state revenue from the top, which benefits only a small percentage of the people, to the bottom in order to benefit the mass majority of North Carolinians."

The audience seemed stunned and there was only an occasional handclap that came from the youngest representatives. Governor Trout hesitated and slowly surveyed the audience before continuing. He lifted his prepared speech and let it drop to the lectern. Staring out to those present he said, "Well, I will not continue the speech I have here for it is even more shocking. I will quickly sum up my intended course of action in the future. I intend to be the Governor for the majority of North Carolinians and will do all in my power to restore their faith in the democracy of this Great State. I will carry out the wishes of the majority and not my wishes. No, it will not be business as usual. My concern will not be directed toward the powerful and affluent of this state. They can, and will, take care of themselves. I will champion the cause of the average Carolinian who pays the bill and is seldom heard. Finally let me say the State of the State of North Carolina is indeed excellent and the lives of the majority of Carolinians will become much improved over the next several years. Thank you ladies and gentlemen."

With this remark the Governor concluded his speech. There was a minimum of applause as he made his way from the speaker's stand. Most of the veteran legislators were not courteous enough to wait and left immediately.

All major North Carolina newspapers carried headline accounts of Governor Trout's radical proposals the following day. The media hounded him for interviews, and there were to be many in the coming months.

The strategy worked and the Governor grabbed the attention of the working majority.

Chapter 21

Carolina Tribune
*"It is my principle that the will of
the majority should always prevail."*
Jefferson

The reaction of those present at the Governor's speech was anticipated and was of little concern to the Governor. The response from the people, however, was vitally important and the Governor and Wadus watched anxiously over the next several weeks trying to determine the impact it had made upon the socio-economic majority.

The Governor was abandoned completely by his party and made a point of emphasizing this fact over the coming year. He and Wadus spent many evenings in the mansion office discussing strategy, answers to opposition, and how to maximize meager campaign funds.

Wadus had been correct and the Governor's enemies attempted to discredit him every way possible. He was called upon to answer for every personal infraction, even for getting caught smoking while in high school as well as having had too much to drink once while in law school. Rumors circulated he had been unfaithful to his wife and that a divorce was imminent. None appeared to do him any damage and small campaign donations began to trickle in as more of his radical proposals were in the media almost daily. The average working Carolinian did not think them so radical and began talking more about Thomas Trout.

There were only a small number of legislators who would support him and most tried to paint him as a North Carolina Huey Long.

The Governor traveled as much as possible visiting the smallest, as well as largest, communities. No group was too small, no person too insignificant, and he came to understand the life and concerns of the average Carolinian.

Wadus put together a small, and easy to understand, packet of information that was widely distributed throughout North Carolina. It said nothing about voting for Tom Trout or the coming election. It detailed very clearly the citizens' rights of initiative, referendum, and recall. Governor Trout spoke much about these little known tools and urged the people to become familiar with them and to use them. He spoke more and more about the concept of democracy and the will of the majority. He constantly told the people to demand elected representatives to serve the will of the greatest number. He reinforced the power of the many over the few. He said, "If they do not serve the majority, recall them, remove them from office. This applies to the Governor as well as all other elected public officials." He urged the people to watch the state budget and to demand accountability for the expenditures of the peoples' money. He asked, "How is it so many legislators arrive in the capitol with meager personal assets, yet after several terms in office are financially well off? Do they become financial geniuses upon arriving in Raleigh? They truly must. The average citizen works all of his life and is lucky to retire with a small pension and social security."

The Governor demanded more and more from inmate 204. Wadus provided him with what farmers, truckers, construction workers, secretaries, teachers, parents, and others wanted to hear. The Governor often used historical illustrations, which Wadus had provided, in order to make a point. In one interview on being questioned concerning his views of the common working citizen he said, "Look, let me tell you a story. Although the ancient Romans introduced the concept of a republic, for the first two hundred years of that republic it was very undemocratic. The average citizen, the plebeian, was ignored because only upper class wealthy patricians were elected to the Roman Senate. You can imagine who benefited from laws passed and who paid the bills. Not really unlike our state and national legislatures are today. Well, after many years of protesting, and with great effort, the plebeians of Rome gained the right to elect ten Tribunes who represented their interests. These Tribunes had great power because if a law was passed by the patrician senate and was unfair to the common man, or plebeian, this Tribune could veto the entire law. It was not long before the Roman Republic became much more democratic and the Senate was forced to be responsive to the problems and needs of the average Roman citizen. Now, I ask you, what would happen across this nation today if the average wage earner, the American plebeian, had the right to elect such an official? One who had the power to veto state and federal laws that placed an unfair burden upon them and granted the wealthy greater advantages and privileges. Can you imagine how responsive all lawmakers would become to the will of the majority if the majority had such a watchdog? Another thing, why would anyone, other than a politician's family, donate huge amounts of money in order to get him elected? There is only one true answer, because it is an investment to insure their continued special privileges. I cannot speak for other states, but I tell you this very clearly and plainly, if I continue as Governor of North Carolina I intend to be the Tribune for the North Carolina plebeians. The average, the working, the struggling common citizen of this state."

This story, and statement, made headline news across N.C. and the Governor began to get more attention from the national new media. By September Thomas Trout not only had the attention of the great majority of Carolinians, and the animosity of the wealthy minority, but was often mentioned across America. He was interviewed on one of the major national talk shows and in early October appeared on the cover of Time magazine in the characterization of a Roman Tribune.

The Governor's enemies became more and more concerned with the growing popularity of the man they had laughed at eight months earlier and called a "hillbilly." Their desperation increased and became more aggressive and vindictive. Wadus and the Governor's daughter became victims.

In an interview in early October a young, brash, reporter asked, "Governor Trout is it true there was an inmate from

Central Prison working at the mansion and is it true your daughter was sexually assaulted by this inmate?"

The Governor reacted as a father and not as the chief executive of North Carolina. The room became very silent as the Governor stared at the reporter and replied, "There is an inmate working in the mansion, he has been there over two years. He is still there. No he did not attack my daughter. Now young man you just crossed the line. All of you had better listen to me." The reporter started to speak and the Governor said, "Shut-up! Don't say another word! You can attack me, what I believe in, what I do, my campaign, but never again attack my family with your muckraking slanderous rumors. If one word appears, in any newspaper or elsewhere, which is a vicious lie and brings one second of grief to my wife or daughter, I promise you before I am done I will own the media you work for. Yes, the inmate is still in the mansion, if that can tell your simple, vindictive, dirty little mind anything. I only wish he could sue you, as an attorney I would gladly represent him. I have come to know him as a trusted and valued friend. All of you best heed what you have heard." He rose and left the room quickly. This incident, or information, never appeared in print.

The Governor was furious. He called Senator Jacob's office. "Senator, I want you to meet me at the mansion at 4:30 today."

"I'm sorry I have another commitment."

"Break it. Be there. It will certainly be to your best interest." He slammed down the phone.

Wadus was working in the Governor's office when he arrived and seeing this man really angry for the first time got up and said, "Sir, I'll go do something else for awhile."

"No, stay here, you're part of this, and I want you to hear it!" Wadus did as instructed and sat silently across the room.

Senator Jacobs entered the office just after 4:30 and the Governor got up and said, "Have a seat Senator. Wadus, close the door please."

Both men sat and Wadus stood quietly to one side of the room as the Governor began. "Senator Jacobs I realize how you feel toward me and also that we are poles apart politically. I also respect the fact you have been in the senate for many years. I accept all of this and have no problem with any of it. However, I do have a problem when someone tries to get at me by slandering my child."

"I have no idea what you are talking about."

"I think you do. I think it either came from you or someone you know. So listen, earlier today a reporter asked me if this inmate had sexually assaulted my daughter. That's a lie. Now understand this senator, tell your people to call off their dogs and never bring up my daughter, or wife, again. You're gonna do this, and do it today, because if you do not I will have Warden White make a statement to the press relating how you tried to use your position to make this man's prison term much harder. Possibly to the point he would be killed." The Senator sat in stunned silence, and Wadus heard the full details for the first time. The Governor continued, "That's right Senator, those media jackals would just love to sink their teeth into that story. Now, Senator, the election is only a few weeks away. I may well be defeated, and I'm sure you are working and praying for such, however, if by some miracle I should be re-elected I will count on your support on some key legislation and programs. I have made the people of N.C. many promises. I will expect, and advise, you to help me keep the major ones. I hope you understand how serious I am. I do regret this dogfight had to sink to such a level, Senator, but it was forced upon me. That's all Senator, good day."

The Senator left quickly without speaking. The Governor said, "Yes, Wadus, I've known about him for some time. Was that Machiavellian enough for you?"

"Yes sir, you even frightened me. But what did he have against me, I've never done him any harm."

"He had nothing against you. The parents of those boys you beat have contributed a great deal of money to his campaigns over the years. In fact, I know exactly how much, but I'll play that card in another game when the stakes are high enough."

"Sir, I certainly hope you win. You have truly learned to be the Governor."

Wadus had not seen his friend Mohamet much over the past months but had told him to call when he had a telephone privilege. It was the third week in October and Mohamet called but not at the usual time.

"Wadus, man I called quick as I could. Something bad's goin down real soon."

Wadus was extremely concerned something had happened at Central and asked, "What has happened to you Mohamet?"

"Nothing's happened to me man. Rumor is that your boss is gonna be hit."

"What in the world are you talking about?"

"Man listen, these cons in here knows cons outside and when something big gonna happin they usually know bout it. The line is the Governor's gonna have a accident. Maybe in that big car, most likely in that chopper he flies round in. Maybe it don't mean nothin, maybe it does. You best tell him to watch his own ass."

"I will, Mohamet, thank you and make sure you stay out of trouble."

Wadus hurried to the Governor's office and called him at the capitol. The secretary answered and he said, "Yes, this is Wilkes Robeson, I need to speak with the Governor immediately." The name was one they had worked out to use if there was ever an emergency or some last minute information he had to get to the Governor.

"Yes sir, Mr. Robeson, he's not here now, but I'll inform him immediately." She called the Governor who was in Cary, N.C. only a short distance from Raleigh. In less than thirty minutes the Governor was speaking to Wadus.

"Sir, I'm sorry but this is important." He related the information and said, "I hope this is all untrue, but don't take any chances. Don't come back in the same vehicle, have a patrol unit drive you back."

"Yes, Mr. Robeson, I understand. Thank you for calling." The Governor arrived back at the mansion in a state patrol unit and went directly to his office where Wadus was waiting.

"Now, Wadus, tell me this again very slowly from the beginning." He listened carefully and asked, "Do you really think these prison rumors have any credence?"

"I don't know, sir, but I know the man it came from, and he can smell danger like a hungry wolf can smell a lamb. I respect his judgement. Do you have any major trips planned between now and election day?"

"I'm supposed to go to Asheville next week."

"How are you traveling?"

"In the state helicopter."

"It might be wise to change your plans at the last possible moment. Also between now and election day always take a different vehicle than you are expected to take."

"Wadus, this sounds pretty far fetched to me, besides the BCI and my security men have seen sticking real close. None of them have any such information."

"That's good, and I hope you are right. But why take the chance?"

The Governor agreed and began to alter his plans at the very last minute. He was driven to Asheville the following week and ordered the state helicopter thoroughly inspected and serviced. When inspected a cupful of plastic explosive was found around a fuel line out of routine sight. This was kept very quiet and the Governor did not even tell his wife. Security was greatly increased and a guard was posted on the vehicles.

October ended and the November election day arrived. Monday night before the election day Governor Trout and his prisoner talked for some time.

"Well Wadus, we've done all we possibly could, and it's almost over. Tomorrow the people speak, and we'll know if we were right or wrong about what they want. It feels good, at least we gave them one hell of a campaign didn't we."

"Yes sir."

"Wadus, I don't know what to say to you. It is impossible to thank you, so I won't try. Grace and I have often talked about you and the impact you have had upon our lives over the past several years. I would not have run for a second term if it had not been for you. But the one thing we are the most grateful for is the difference you made in our daughter's life. Sometimes I feel a little jealous and think she loves you more than me, and of course, you can shag and taught her how. I couldn't. I can't sum everything up, but someday I hope to write it all up. If we're not here after this term we'll stay in touch, and I'll do all I possibly can to help you. We still have many questions about you, questions we can't answer, but just the same I feel there's something about you maybe no one can explain."

"Sir, I don't know those answers myself. I wish I did! It took me several years to realize the first Wadus Strickland died with his son in 1988. I just don't know about the second Wadus Strickland. Anyway, this house, and all in it have become part of whatever I am now. I've already been paid. Good night sir."

The following day North Carolinians voted in record numbers. It was one of those days that never seems to end, but finally the sun went down and the polls closed. Governor Trout, Grace, and Wadus watched the score as the numbers came in. By the eleven o'clock news hour it was evident that Thomas C. Trout had been re-elected by a sound majority. The Trouts, and Wadus Strickland, would share the same residence for at least the coming four years.

Chapter 22

Franklin's Purse

"A politician thinks of the next election;
a statesman, of the next generation."
James Freeman Clarke

Debra Trout had finished high school in June, admitted to the University of North Carolina, and wanted to become an attorney like her father. Wadus missed her and looked forward to the weekends she came home. She kept him informed of even the smallest details of her life in Chapel Hill including the boys that she had little time for but talked about anyway. She was a determined young lady and vowed she would finish her undergraduate studies in three years that meant attending summer sessions. Wadus was impressed, and as always, listened and occasionally offered suggestions. She was goal oriented and in a hurry to get into law school. She always insisted upon pulling the ping pong dance floor from beneath the bed and shagging to several tunes. Wadus found it more and more difficult to keep up with her seemingly inexhaustible energy. After shagging on one of her trips home Wadus said, "You know, Honey, I suppose I should get that old ping pong board out of here."

Debra reacted as if he intended to rob her and exclaimed, "Don't you dare Wadus. I love that board and I intend to have it always even when Dad is no longer Governor. You don't know how much that old board means to me." She smiled and said, "You'll help me steal it when we leave won't you, Wadus?"

"Honey, are you trying to get me more time? I think I have enough already."

"Don't worry about it, by then I'll be an attorney and won't let anything happen to you."

"Now that's a real comfort."

Wadus could not help but remember his Jamie every time she came home. He thought of his son in college, the activities, the studies, and the young ladies like Debra his boy never had a chance to enjoy. His heart seemed to ache more, rather than less, and he prayed for some miracle to enable him to endure his remaining years.

Governor Trout wasted little time in proving his campaign promises. He had told Wadus, "The easy part is over, now the real work begins. Wadus, I think the best thing I can do for this state is to try to make sure every child gets a much better education. So, let's start with the lottery issue. Franklin once said, 'If a man empties his purse into his head, no one can take it from him,' and I intend to do just that for the next generation of North Carolinians."

They quickly put a plan into operation that had been worked out months earlier. A plan to determine if N.C. would have a state lottery. The Governor announced it to the people and news media on February 12, 1993.

"I have promised you, and myself, to do the will of the majority of Carolinians. We shall begin with the question of whether or not this state shall have a lottery. This will not be decided by me, or the legislature, but by a vote of the people of this State. If rejected, I shall be satisfied for you have spoken. If accepted, all revenue raised will be added to the educational budget and used solely for education. I have one vote and I shall vote my conscience. I hope all others will do the same after carefully examining theirs. Thousands of devoutly religious persons are against a lottery for they say it is gambling. Yet, many of these very ones first turn to the financial section of the morning paper to determine how their stocks did on the market yesterday. Many churches often sell tickets on raffles in order to raise money for worthwhile Christian projects. That is good. I hope to sell N.C. lottery tickets to raise money for a very good project. To better educate every child in this state so he may look forward to a better life than his parents have had. Isn't this also a Christian goal? The God I believe in, and love, also loves children, and I further believe He will bless those who do all they can for the children. Nevertheless, the majority will decide. I have established a committee in each of N.C.s' 100 counties. Tomorrow's newspapers will carry a list of names to contact in each county. These are petition committees and will circulate petitions throughout each county in every community. If you want this decided by referendum sign one of these petitions. As soon as the required number has signed we shall work toward a date to decide the issue. Either way the vote goes I only hope that the majority does turn out to vote, for the majority will prevail. There will be other important questions decided by you the people over the next several years. This same organization, and system, will be used."

Petitions were indeed signed by far more than was required. A date was set for a vote and the populace responded in record numbers to having been "asked."

The lottery passed by a 67 percent majority, and by the end of 1993 tickets were being sold across the state. Funds for education began to grow. Money previously spent by Carolinians on the Virginia lottery stayed at home to help the children of North Carolina. Most said it was well worth a dollar just for a brief beautiful dream not to mention the good cause. Some had their dream come true.

Wadus and the Governor kept a secret score board, a plan, for major goals. The Tribune did indeed veto many pork bills and was applauded by most taxpayers. Nothing succeeds like success, and although many legislators hated Tom Trout they could not ignore his popularity among their constituents. Many were forced, against their will, to support some of his programs. Even Senator Jacobs gave lip service of approval.

The lottery was a tremendous success, and within a year schools across the state were reaping the benefits. Children in small, isolated, mountain schools and elsewhere, who only had radios in their homes now sat in front of computers. Books, materials, better and free lunches, were provided, and the Governor encouraged each school to expose the children to other areas of the state through school sponsored travel. Teachers' salaries were greatly increased as was their accountability and responsibility. A bill became law requiring all to receive a master's degree within seven years.

The Governor traveled the state visiting as many schools as possible for a first hand appraisal and enjoyed the children more and more. He would often stop at a small school and enter unannounced to talk briefly with children and teachers. He always tried to sample the free school lunch to determine its quality. One Friday evening as he traveled back to Raleigh from the eastern coastal plain he saw the lights of a football field near a very large high school. He told the driver to go to the stadium. He walked through the gates and down the sideline followed by four state troopers and two BCI agents. It was half time and the activities were coming to an end as the Governor spoke with a coach. As the band stopped, the coach and the Governor walked to the microphone on the field. The coach spoke, "Ladies and gentlemen, especially students, we have a surprise visitor. The Governor of the Great State of North Carolina, Governor Thomas C. Trout."

Everyone stood and it was some time before the applause quieted and the Governor said, "Please forgive me for interrupting your game, but as we were passing I saw your beautiful school, the lights, and couldn't resist them. I will be very brief. I have only two questions for students present. One, is your school better than it has ever been?" The uproar was unbelievable and lasted some time. The Governor continued and said, "Second question. Is it getting even better?" Again there was a great and positive response and the Governor said, "I speak now directly to the students. It is up to you. Your parents, teachers, and the taxpayers of N.C. are determined to provide you with great opportunity. Don't let them down, use every minute, every advantage, to develop the full potential which God has granted you. Only you can do that and it is all up to you now. We all look forward to great accomplishments from you in the years to come. Now, thank you so very much, and may the best team win." He walked from the field shaking hands and enjoying the thunderous noise of approval as he returned to his vehicle and continued on to Raleigh.

The Governor and Wadus outlined their objectives for tax reform. It took almost three years, convincing argument and some political intimidation, but he finally pushed through a tax law that favored families earning less than $35,000 per year. They would pay zero state income tax. Children from low-income families were guaranteed a college scholarship if they maintained a high academic average in high school. He was able to push for a bill exempting retired persons over sixty-five from paying a state income tax on their pensions.

People earning an hourly wage were relieved from state income tax on all hours over forty per week. The results of this were immediate and amazing. Many worked more overtime, had more money, purchased more consumer goods, and more tax paying jobs were created and on and on.

The Governor talked about eliminating state income taxes altogether as Florida and Nevada had done. He could not get any support on this whatsoever. He was able eventually to eliminate the sales tax on food. There were a number of bills that greatly increased taxes on families earning over one hundred thousand dollars per year. Many loopholes for the wealthy were swept away. He answered his critics by saying, "Remember the North Carolina State poem. 'Where the weak grow strong, and the strong grow great,' I believe in that. The strong, and the wealthy, can take care of themselves. They need no help. The weak do, and I want to help the weak grow strong. By becoming strong they will push the already strong to even greater strength and wealth. Those at the top don't seem to understand this logic, and once at the top they want to pull the ladder up behind them."

There were many outstanding accomplishments, and some defeats, for the Governor over the next three years, but he was truly the peoples' Governor and Tribune. Wadus Strickland, still unknown and unseen, walked every step of this political road with Tom Trout. It demanded a heavy toll from each man, but at least Wadus was spared the strain of travel, public office, and constantly answering to the media.

Late one evening in the fall of 1994 as Wadus and the Governor were finishing for the night the Governor said, "God, I'm so tired, I wish there were some place Grace and I could go where nobody knows us and we could be totally alone. Just eat and sleep for a few days. But that's only wishful thinking."

"Not really, I think it could be done."

"How?"

"It would have to be very secretive, you wouldn't have your security, and you would actually have to slip out of here. You would also need a different automobile and have to drive yourself. But, if you really want what you just described, I have a small place on the coast where you would be alone and completely undisturbed."

Governor Trout sat up quickly and said, "Wadus, you amaze me. What am I going to discover next about you? Yes, I am very interested. You know, Wadus, in a way I'm just as much a prisoner as you. If you're serious I'll talk to Grace. Just the thought of being a normal person for a couple of days is exciting." He did talk to his wife, and she was equally as excited and several nights later the three conspired and planned the escape in the mansion office.

It was difficult for Wadus not to laugh because they whispered and acted as two teenagers who were planning to sneak out of their parents' home for an adventurous evening out.

Mrs. Trout asked, "What about a car? We can't use the state vehicles and if I rent one it'll be all over Raleigh in two hours."

"I think Ms. Clark can be trusted and would probably loan you hers."

They looked at each other and the Governor said, "Yes I'll bet she would."

Wadus drew a detailed map of how to get to his cottage. He gave them the number and said, "Before you arrive call this number and say, "Wadus said I should call you," the man will meet you at the cottage. He will never mention to anyone that you are there. He will also go get anything you might need. Unless you get out, and ride around a lot, no one will ever know who's in the house." All was finally arranged. Wadus told Ms. Clark of the conspiracy, and she was excited and glad to help. On Thursday, after dark, Mrs. Trout drove through the mansion gates while her husband hid in the back seat. The officer at the gate assumed it to be Ms. Clark and in the dim light paid little attention and only waved. A few miles away Mrs. Trout stopped, and her husband drove toward the coast. Their contact was waiting and showed them in. He then went and purchased a list of food items they needed. The Governor and his wife returned late the following Sunday. Their trip had been just the regeneration both had needed.

Wadus spent occasional weekends at Central in cell 101. Mohamet continued his pursuit of knowledge. He had read many books and especially enjoyed biographies of historical persons. He depended upon Wadus only to provide a name, a direction, then he would read all the prison library had to offer. The men talked more about Mohamet's possibilities of parole, but the black man had little hope in acquiring freedom for many years to come.

Over the years Wadus realized how much Ms. Clark's attention, and occasional contact, had lifted his burden and given him something wonderful to at least think about. They had been alone many times, had kissed only a few, and had talked a great deal. He continued to encourage her to see the reality of their vastly different worlds and to realize how she was wasting precious time thinking of him as the man in her life. She would become upset and would not hear anything except what she dreamed of. She took her vacation each year and went to the coast and stayed in the cottage. She never revealed this to the Governor and would only listen when they told her what a wonderfully peaceful place it was and how much they had enjoyed their brief stay there.

Debra Trout finished her undergraduate degree on schedule in August of 1995. She had coerced her father into bringing inmate 204 to the graduation exercise in Chapel Hill. Wadus held his hands close together and tried to conceal the handcuffs by tucking them under each coat sleeve. He proudly watched this young lady receive her college degree. After the ceremony she ran and embraced her father, mother, and turned to Wadus and threw her arms tightly around him and began to cry tears of joy. She entered law school at UNC two weeks later.

Chapter 23

Sunset Or Dawn

"There is a divinity that shapes our ends,
Rough-hew them how we will."
Shakespeare-*Hamlet*

It was October 19, 1995, a Thursday and one of the many gorgeous autumn days Carolina is famous for. The day had been routine for Wadus. He had spent some time in the kitchen, finished a few things in the Governor's office, talked with Ms. Clark for some time, and had even walked around outside to enjoy the blue sky and fall colors.

The Governor arrived at the mansion around 4:00 that afternoon. He told a staff member to send Wadus to his office immediately. This was not unusual, and Wadus thought no more of it than the hundreds of other times he had received the same order.

The Governor sat behind his desk looking through papers as Wadus entered and said, "Yes sir."

The Governor looked up quickly and sternly said, "Strickland, go to your room and pack what things you have. You are going back to Central. There is a patrol unit waiting out front for you."

Wadus was so stunned and overwhelmed he stood as if frozen. He finally raised his arms slightly and said, "Sir I don't—," but was not allowed to continue.

"Never mind the questions, just do as told, get your things together, you're going back to Central."

Wadus turned slowly and began to make his way to his small room as if sleepwalking. He closed the door and sat on the side of his bed. He lowered his head and searched his mind for an explanation but could not find one. After sometime he pulled a small brown suitcase from beneath his bed. There was not much to pack. He carefully folded, and packed all the clothing Ms. Clark had given him, and his razor, toothbrush, and a large thick brown envelope. He thought of Ms. Clark as he took off his white waistcoat, folded it neatly, and laid it on the bed. He hoped he could slip through the kitchen without anyone noticing the suitcase. He took several deep breaths, picked-up the suitcase, and walked from the room closing the door behind him. He hesitated and stared at the closed door for several moments. Shaking his head he turned and made his way to the kitchen. No one was there, and though unusual, he was very grateful and moved on. He made his way toward the main entrance and seeing the Governor standing near the door he stopped and said, "Sir, I'll go out the back way," and started to turn around.

"No, go out this front entrance, come on."

Wadus obeyed and upon entering the area turned and looked down the corridor. Everyone was there. Mrs. Trout, Debra, the entire kitchen staff, and Jefferson were watching him. Mrs. Trout walked and stood beside the Governor as he said, "Come on, Wadus, we're not going to bite you." Wadus approached the Governor in total confusion until he stood facing him.

Governor Trout handed Wadus an envelope and said, "My dear friend, you must go back to Central tonight because you will be processed out early tomorrow morning. You are a free man! This is a full and complete pardon."

Wadus took the envelope as everyone clapped and shouted. He could not speak and tears rolled down each side of his face. Debra began to cry and threw her arms around his neck and said, "Oh Wadus, we love you so much."

"I love you too Honey."

The staff came forward, congratulating and shaking his hand. Shawna embraced him and said, "Wadus, my main man, now we gonna do some real shaggin at the beach, right."

"Right Shawna; you got it."

185

Mrs. Clara was the last and Wadus walked to her, looked down into her big, beautiful, wise face, and putting his arms around her said, "Mrs. Clara, I love you and I'll never forget all the kindness you have shown me. I wish I could—."

"Yo hush now, Snowball. I lovs yo to an knows yo ah good man. Yo gonna be jus fine. Da Lawd is wit yo Snowball. Jus don't yo fogat bout Mrs. Clara, yo hear."

"No ma'am, I never will."

The staff left and the Governor, Mrs. Trout, and Debra all tried to talk at the same time.

"Wadus, I've got to go, but as soon as you get settled call me at school and give me your telephone number and address. I'll be seeing you soon and you can show me some of those beach clubs. I can't wait. Bye now."

Mrs. Trout said, "Wadus Srickland, you are still my mystery man and you aren't leaving without this." She reached out putting both hands on his cheeks and gave him a serious kiss on the lips. The Governor looked as if he couldn't believe her as she said, "That was for me, and for all you have done for Tom, Debra, and myself. Good luck Wadus."

Wadus was embarrassed and replied, "Thank you ma'am."

The Governor took another envelope from his coat and said, "Wadus, it isn't possible for me to pay you for what you have meant to me, and this isn't meant as payment. There's fifteen hundred dollars here to help get you home and maybe for a few things you'll need."

"Governor, I appreciate the thought and your kindness, but I don't need it sir."

"Don't need it, why not?"

"Well, my teacher's pension has been invested for me for the last seven years and I've been extremely lucky."

"Wadus, you are something else"

"Remember sir, it's a poor dog that doesn't bury a bone. There are a couple of things I would ask of you and would be very grateful for." He bent down, opened the suitcase, took out a large brown envelope and handed it to the Governor. "The first is I would ask that you file this and take care of everything in the event something happens to me. It is a will and some other legal papers. Secondly, sir, if it is possible I ask that you use your influence in order to have my cellmate, Mohamet

186

Kabul's, case and record reviewed by the Attorney General. Sir, he is a different man now, a good man, and is the man who may have saved your life."

Mrs. Trout looked curiously at her husband as he said, "I'll review everything and see what can be done."

Wadus said good bye and walked out the door and made his way toward the waiting patrol unit. He could only think, and wonder, why Trina had not been present.

The trooper opened the rear door and Wadus started to get in but was stopped by Ms. Clark's voice as she approached the vehicle. "Wadus, wait a minute."

As she came near he extended his hand only to have it slapped away as she threw her arms around his neck and said, "Forget that." She kissed him long and passionately.

Wadus was finally able to say, "Trina, the Governor, Mrs. Trout, and everybody's watching."

"Good! Now they know." She pressed a key into his hand and said, "Wadus, please be here tomorrow night. Don't say anything, I couldn't take it. I'll be there at seven, leave the door unlocked. If it is locked I'll know you aren't there and what it means. You are a free man now, I can't hold you captive any longer. Just remember, there or not, I love you Wadus Strickland." She turned and walked toward her car to leave for the day.

Wadus entered the patrol unit and was driven away as the Governor and Mrs. Trout watched what had taken place with great interest.

"My God, Grace, did you see that? What's been going on here all this time anyway?"

"Not what you think."

"Right, and I didn't see what I just saw."

"Oh she loves him alright, but they have never made love."

"Now, just how do you know that pray tell?"

"Cause I'm from Venus and you're from Mars."

The Governor embraced his wife and said, "Is that right. Well, Miss Venus you better get ready to see a different galaxy tonight."

Mrs. Trout laughed and said, "I hope that's a promise Governor."

"You got it, it's an executive order."

As the patrol unit made its way to Central, Wadus studied the key and thought of what Trina had said. He recognized the name of the hotel but had never been a guest there. It was the most luxurious and expensive in Raleigh and often used by the wealthy, politicians, and socialites. He put the key into his small suitcase. His bag was taken away on arrival and he was escorted to the Warden's office.

As Wadus entered his office the Warden walked over, extended his hand and said, "Congratulations Strickland, have a seat." The Warden was extremely pleasant as he explained the releasing procedure to take place the following morning. He finally said; "Well Wadus, this is the last time we will talk, so I want you to know I am sincerely happy for you. Frankly, you should have never been here in the first place. How long has it been?"

"Just over seven years, sir." They shook hands again and Wadus was taken to cell 101 for his last night as an inmate. As the door opened and he stepped into the cell Mohamet jumped to his feet and asked, "Man what's happened?"

"I've been pardoned by the Governor! Starting tomorrow I'm a free man!"

Mohamet gave him an almost crushing hug and said, "Praise Allah, praise Allah! Man you made it."

The two men talked well into the night. The following morning Wadus ate his last meal in Central with his friend. As they passed through the serving line one of the inmates serving food said, "Hey Mohamet, you got your lady back man."

Mohamet stared down at the inmate and said, "Shut up you hedonistic vermin."

As they moved on the inmate serving asked another, "Hey man, what did he call me?"

"Man he said you give head ta all da men."

Wadus laughed as he realized how far his friend had come and was quite sure he was now well educated.

Wadus said good bye to Mohamet and upon parting added, "Now listen carefully friend, don't make any mistakes. I still see you outside, and things are going to be done. If possible you will be free. Remember, trust me, think, think, and then think some more. Don't screw-up, no matter what." They embraced again and Mohamet watched the small white man, whom he had wanted to kill seven years earlier, walk out of his life. He stood silent and dealt with his great feeling of emptiness and depression. He said, "Good bye, Brother, Allah Akbar."

Wadus was processed out and given what things he had on him the day of the accident plus the suitcase. He received his beautiful masonic ring, wallet containing sixty dollars, shoes, belt, shirt and trousers. He was led to the main entrance and the gates were opened. As he walked through them into the bright morning sun, and freedom, he heard someone call to him from behind. He turned to see one of the officers who had beaten him approaching.

"Mr. Strickland, please wait a minute, I'd like to say something if you'll let me?"

"Of course, what is it?"

"I'm one of the men who beat you, and I want to ask you to forgive me. I wouldn't blame you if you didn't, but I had to ask and also to say I'm sorry."

"I know, son. I forgave you that night. Don't worry, I know you're a good man, and it was worth it to get that man to come out."

"I'll never forget you and that night in the Warden's office. Whenever I get angry with someone, in here or outside, I think of you, and it's easy to forgive him. Good luck, sir."

"Thank you son, take care of yourself." He watched as the officer returned and the gates closed. He stared at the gates and walls for sometime before turning and walking away.

A large man got out of a car some distance away and called, "Wadus."

Wadus stopped and recognizing Captain Stewart walked to him and said, "Hello Captain, what are you doing here?"

"I have friends inside and heard the good news yesterday. I thought you might need a ride somewhere. Are you going to Smithfield? I'll be glad to give you a ride."

"No sir, not today. I've got to see a man here for a few hours, then I don't know where I'll go."

"Well, get in, and I'll drop you off."

Wadus got into the car and gave the Captain the address. As they drove the Captain said, "You know I've been retired for a couple of years, but I try to keep up with things in the department."

The automobile stopped at its destination and the captain asked, "Are you sure this is the right place? These are the offices of the most prominent CPA in Raleigh."

"Yes sir, it's the right place. Thank you so much and I hope everything goes well for you in your retirement."

The captain said good bye and drove away as Wadus entered the building. He approached the receptionist and said, "My name is Wadus Strickland; I'd like to see Mr. Martin." The secretary called that office, and a door quickly open down the hallway as a small man hurried toward him.

The CPA began shaking Wadus's hand vigorously and said, "My God, Wadus, it's good to see you. Come in my office we've got a lot to talk about." He looked at the secretary and said, "No calls, I don't want to be disturbed."

After entering the office and talking for almost an hour the CPA said, "Well, Wadus, let's see how you stand." He went to the files and returned with a thick folder. Handing Wadus a single sheet he said, "We'll go over the entire portfolio, but this is the bottom line as of several weeks ago."

Wadus studied the balance sheet and gazed upon the number at the bottom. He looked up and asked, "Martin are these figures correct?"

Showing a great smile of satisfaction the CPA said, "Absolutely Wadus. The market has been really good for you, and the so-called 8th miracle has worked wonders. You have to remember your pension, with the exception of the small amount sent for house cleaning, has been invested each month and nothing has been touched. The way I have it set up, with your monthly pension and the interest from this amount, you will have a gross income of at least $100,000 per year. That's without touching this amount!"

"I don't know what to say. God, this is hard to believe." Looking further Wadus asked, "Where is the figure for your fee? I don't see it anywhere."

"Don't insult me friend. Just buy me a round of golf at the coast, and we'll call it my fee." The CPA went to a safe, returned and handed Wadus money and said, "There's $3,000 there, it should get you home and do until I can establish an account there for you."

When Wadus told his friend he already had a room for that night and where his friend replied, "Damn Wadus, maybe I should have given you more money. Do you know how much that place charges?"

"No, but it has already been taken care of."

"Oh I see, that's different." He let Wadus out in front of this fine hotel and drove away. Wadus looked up at the tower of floors and then up and down the street. He crossed the street and sat on a bus stop bench as he continued to look at the huge structure and the key he held in his hand. He remembered the day Trina Clark had first walked into the mansion kitchen, that wonderful day in her office, the sound of her voice, her smell, her winks and pinches, their talks. He thought of them all and was afraid. He thought, "I can't go into that building; I can't ask or expect such a woman to be mine." He told himself he should walk away and never look back. He realized it was impossible for him to do, arose, crossed the street and entered the hotel.

He went to the elevator and to the top floor. He unlocked the door and entered a beautiful suite. It had a huge kitchen, breakfast room, sitting room, an extremely large bedroom and a bathroom as large as his mansion quarters. There was a wet bar and refrigerator. Beside a large bowl of fruit there was a bottle of Black Velvet and a bottle of very good zinfandel wine. A note read, "Please put the wine in the refrigerator." and he did.

He took a bath in the huge tub, shaved, and put on the clothes Trina Clark had given him. It was 6:40, he poured himself a drink, sat and looked out over the city of Raleigh. He mixed another at 7:05 and at 7:15 began to imagine Trina had begun to re-evaluate her future when the door slowly and quietly opened. He stood and faced her. She closed the door and faced him as if afraid to to come any further. She was more beautiful than he ever remembered, or imagined, a woman could be. She wore a sleek low-cut black dress slightly cut up each side and she wore high heel shoes. She was dressed for the opera, or at least a fine dinner at some exclusive and elegant club.

Neither spoke. She walked slowly to him, placed her forehead on his chest, and began to softly cry as she said, "Oh Wadus, I've been standing outside for 20 minutes. I couldn't get enough nerve to turn the knob. I was so afraid it would be locked and you wouldn't be here. Oh, Wadus, just hold me."

He held her gently and said, "Shssssssss, everything's fine, don't cry darling." She looked up, and he held her beautiful face in his hands and kissed her passionately for at least 15 seconds and then began to kiss away her tears with easy light kisses and said, "You're even beautiful when you're crying."

They held on to each other for a long time enjoying the freedom to feel, and share, without fear. He said, "Trina, lock the door please."

She looked up, giggled as she wiped her eyes and said, "I think I've heard that line before." She locked the door and returned as Wadus was opening the wine. She wrapped her arms around him from behind as he poured a glass of wine, turned and gave it to her. They took their glasses, walked to the large windows, and held each other as they watched the beautiful orange sunset.

After two glasses of wine, the tears and fears were gone. She talked joyously as she sat on her knees with arms on his legs as he stared down at her and was content to just listen. Her energy was like a cool breeze blowing through his head on a hot afternoon; her voice and words were candy to his ears. She finally asked, "Wadus, do I talk too much? I do don't I. I bet you think I'm silly."

Wadus chuckled, bent forward, kissed her gently on the lips and said, "No, No, and No. I just can't imagine how you have escaped the male population. It just doesn't figure; it isn't logical; doesn't seem possible."

She stood up in front of him and drew his head to her soft stomach, took his hands and placed them on her buttocks and said, "I did escape, it was easy. I just thought of you. That I am yours, and you are mine. Mister Wadus, I'm really kind of old fashioned, so you don't make this redhead jealous, you hear." She poured her fourth glass of wine and he mixed himself another B.V., soda, and lime. It was now dark outside and the only light came from the doorway and the large windows where she now stood. She said, "Wadus, would you come here and unzip me please."

Wadus walked up behind her, slowly unzipped the dress, and backed away a few feet. She did not turn as she pushed the dress over her shoulders and let it fall to the floor. She said, "Dream of mine, you have a right to view the merchandise. It may not be what you want." She turned slowly and faced him. She wore only a narrow black bra and black bikini panties.

Wadus gazed upon the most beautiful female body he had ever seen. He felt a little spasm in his stomach, slightly dizzy, and thought it might be the drinks but knew it was what stood before him. She smiled and asked, "Well do you approve, or are you going to throw me back?"

"Yes, and no. I'm not gonna throw you back. Just let me sit down a minute to make sure I'm not dreaming. Let me catch my breath."

As he sat down she began to laugh, rushed over, bent down, pushed his legs apart, and put her arms around him tightly. After sometime he said, "Trina, I think my heart has slowed down some now, would you fix me another cocktail please." She walked to the bar and he thought her movements and body were as beautiful and graceful as an Arabian stallion. Da Vinci would have loved her.

He walked to her, raised her long hair and began kissing the back of her ears, neck, shoulders, and worked his way slowly down her back and long legs. She trembled, flinched, and breathed faster and faster. He stood, she turned and began to take his trousers off. He continued the spider kisses around her face and neck as he removed her bra and kissed her breasts running his tongue lightly around her beautiful nipples. She moaned and quivered as he bent to his knees lowering her panties. He kissed her stomach and massaged her buttocks, she moaned deeply with a body spasm and wilted to the thick carpet saying, "Oh Wadus, Oh Wadus." He continued kissing her legs, the inside of her thighs and as his hot breath was felt upon her vagina she screamed slightly, trembled and said, "Oh Wadus, I've had two orgasms, please enter my body." She pulled him down as she took his penis and guided it into her body. He entered her deeply variating his thrusts until they both trembled, moaned several times as he felt all of his manhood rush from his body into hers. They lay still, breathed rapidly and held on to each other as if separate metals had been forged together in a hot furnace. He remained on top of her for some time as she said, "Wadus, don't move." As her breathing slowed she whispered, "I did not think I could love you more than I did, I was wrong. I don't know what I'll do now. I had three orgasms, you made it too didn't you?"

"Yes, I certainly did darling, I don't think there's anything left in me." They remained on the carpet, naked in the light from the windows, talked a long time and finished their drinks.

"Wadus, I'm hungry now. Let's go get something to eat."

"It's probably too late to call room service, so we'll have to go out. Let's take a bath in that big tub first O.K."

Trina giggled and said, "Great idea."

They filled the tub and spent an hour talking and bathing each other. They dressed and went down the elevator. Several men entered on the sixth floor and one looked at her and said, "Hello Ms. Clark. Are you at a meeting here tonight."

."No Senator, I'm not."

"Are you staying here tonight?"

Trina took Wadus by the hand and replied, "Yes sir, we have a suite on the top floor."

"Oh I see. Well it's nice to see you."

They found a diner open and had eggs, grits, ham, and coffee. Returning to the suite they went to bed and made love again, slower, but equally as passionate as the first time. She said, "Wadus, I love you more than you'll ever know. Good night."

"I love you too Baby."

They fell asleep holding on to each other as if an elusive fantasy might escape. The following morning Wadus called room service and ordered a gigantic breakfast. By the time it arrived Trina had bathed, dressed, and looked as if she had just arrived. They ate breakfast and talked of many things.

She finally became very serious and said, "Wadus, I have to leave shortly, so I need to say something. Please don't interrupt. I know you have something on your mind, something's eating at you, and I know you will be going to the coast." She took his hand, squeezed and continued, "When you've done what you must do, when you're complete, when you want me, just call. I'll wait, and I'll come. I'll walk out immediately. I love you that much. But I won't come for a night, a weekend, and I won't stay as Trina Clark. Think about this darling; I'll love you always, but if you don't want the same, don't call. I'll never contact you again. I love you too much not to have you completely." She got up, walked around the table, kissed him long and tenderly, and then walked out without looking back or saying anything more. Wadus sat in silence for a long time. He thought of many things; his Jamie, his age, her age, being an ex con, of Mohamet, and he could not find an adequate answer to any of the questions which troubled his mind.

Wadus checked out of the hotel and walked several blocks to the bus station where he purchased a ticket to Smithfield, North Carolina. The bus left at 3 p.m. going south on Int. 40. It took the Smithfield exit at 3:45 and Wadus took his bag, went to the front and said, "I'd like to get off about 5 miles from here. I'll show you where." The driver nodded he understood. Wadus soon indicated the spot. The bus stopped and he got off.

It was October 20th and the day was bright without a cloud in the sky as he began to walk up the rural county road leading to where his son was buried. He walked about a mile and a half before reaching the field he had not seen in over seven years. The field had been mowed and he could see the small stone catching the evening sun far up the hill. As he walked up the hill he could hear the engine of a combine some distance up the road. He approached the stone, stood and looked for a long time. He sat down on his suitcase next to the grave and began to talk.

"Son, this is Dad. I haven't been able to come for a long time, but I guess you know that. Son, when I was last here I hoped we would be together long before now, but for some reason I'm still here. I don't know why. So much has happened over the last seven years and I don't understand any of it. I know you are waiting, but I know you know the feelings I have now and understand. You are 20 years old now and think as a man. I love you more than ever, and miss you more everyday, but I think you know why I must stay. God will surely bring us together eventually, and it is not my place to alter his plan. I don't know what His plan is, and I am sure you know more than I. I love you Jamie and I will find you someday."

Wadus pulled weeds from around the stone and lay down beside it to watch as the sun descended. At 6:30 he got up, said goodbye to his son, walked down the hill and onto the road. He walked toward the bright setting sun on the right side of the road leading back to Rt. 212.

The farmer had finished his day of combining and drove his pickup truck homeward in the same direction Wadus walked. Wadus could hear the truck engine in the distance behind him as the engine noise grew louder. He stepped a few feet off of the road as he continued his journey. It was difficult for the farmer to see as he drove into the sun and he held his hand in front of his eyes. The truck came closer and louder behind Wadus and he heard the tire drop off the pavement onto the shoulder of the road close behind him. He turned just to see the blur of the truck as it struck. He was hurled into the ditch as his suitcase became airborne. The truck slid to a halt and the farmer rushed back hysterically shouting, "Oh my God I didn't see you! Oh my God I'm sorry, please Lord! Are you hurt bad man?"

After some time Wadus slowly opened his eyes and said, "I'm alive man, calm down."

He realized the farmer was holding him as he heard him exclaim, "Thank God, praise Jesus, you're alive. Just be still, I'll call for help."

"No, just let me get my breath, man."

After some time the farmer helped him get to his feet and walked him toward the pickup. Wadus leaned against the truck as the farmer talked frantically.

"I think you just missed me, but I'm pretty sure you killed my suitcase. I just bounced off the side of your truck."

"You stand right here. I'll get it." He hurried to gather the suitcase and its contents. He returned, put the battered case in the back, and helped Wadus into the truck. He wanted to take Wadus to the hospital, but Wadus refused.

"No, no, it's alright. Just take me to the Smithfield bus station."

"Man, I don't know you, but you're going home with me." The farmer drove to his home. He and his wife helped Wadus to a bed and he was soon asleep. He opened his eyes early the following morning and looked into the face of an elderly doctor.

"I've examined you fellow and there's no bones broken. I can't be sure but I don't think you have any internal injuries, but you should go to the hospital for some x-rays and further tests. Do I know you, you look familiar?"

"No, you don't know me. I'll be O.K., I'm just a little sore."

"Well, that's up to you."

The farmer's wife fixed a nice breakfast, and they both pleaded with Wadus to stay with them for a few days just to be sure he was alright. He refused their kind offer and asked the farmer to take him to the Smithfield bus depot. There he purchased a ticket to Shallotte, N.C. and a little past noon was en route. The bus arrived in Shallotte just before 6 p.m., and he hired a taxi to take him to his cottage near Sunset Beach. As the cab driver drove away Wadus looked through his wallet hoping to find the spare key he always kept. It was still there, and he entered his home for the first time in over seven years. He was finally back in his small kingdom by the sea. He went straight to his bedroom and to bed where he would spend most of his time for several days as his aching body healed.

Wadus spent the coming weeks enjoying his little cottage and taking long walks on the beach. He stood for long periods of time staring out on the ocean. It was as though he saw the face and heard the voice of nature. He searched his mind, and conscience, for direction. He spent many late hours in the cozy lounge of the Italian Fisherman Restaurant just watching the archaic swing bridge open, and close, as it let boats pass on the intercoastal waterway. He was on the beach as the sun rose on Friday, November 17th and watched this magnificent event and was grateful God had given him another day to witness His wondrous creations. The sun climbed upward, and he felt as though it spoke to him providing the answer he sought. He went to his vehicle and returned to his cottage.

At 10:30 a.m. he dialed the supervisor's office in the Governor's mansion.

"Hello, Ms. Clark speaking."

"Good morning, Ms. Clark, how are you?"

Ms. Clark stood up quickly, "Wadus is this you?" She began to cry saying, "I had almost given up hope you would call. Wadus, please tell me the truth, but I do hope it is what I pray to hear."

"So do I. Are you ready to come?"

She screamed, "Yes, Oh yes, I'm ready, when do you want me to come? I told the Governor over four weeks ago I might be leaving but that's all I told him. When, Wadus, when?"

"Go to your place, get your clothes, and come now." She talked so fast, and asked so many quick questions Wadus said, "Slow down, Baby, we'll talk about everything after you get here. When can you leave?"

"I'll be on the road by one this afternoon."

"Be careful. Now, you should be here around five. Come to Sunset Beach. I'll be near the pier or walking to the north of it. There aren't many around this time of year so don't worry about finding me. Trina, be careful and I'll see you around five."

"Wadus, I love you, I love you, I love you, and I'm on my way. Good bye." She ran to the kitchen screaming and threw her arms around Mrs. Clara, and as tears flowed she rapidly told her Wadus had called and she was leaving. She said good bye, kissed Mrs. Clara, and ran from the mansion to her car.

Shawna asked, "What did she mean Wadus called and that she's leaving? Where's she goin? That white woman has always acted strange ta me."

"Shawna, I is told yo many ah times dat yo wuz blind as ah bat. Don't yo ever know nothin, don't yo ever sees nothin? Chil yo is pitiful. My, my."

The sun was bright, the wind was cold, and only a few walked on the beach in the late afternoon. Wadus had arrived and walked slowly to the north deep in many thoughts of what he was about to begin. He walked further than he had realized. He glanced at his watch seeing it was 5:30 and turned to start back. He walked only a short distance and saw her about 500 yards away as she jogged toward him.

Trina slowed to a fast walk as she stared at the figure in the distance. He wore a long Australian outback coat, and his long hair whipped about in the strong wind. Realizing it was him she began running toward him shouting, "Wadus, Wadus." He opened his arms as she rushed forward and upon reaching him leaped as she threw both arms around his neck and legs around his body. She began kissing him again and again as he spun her around several times before they fell to the sand still embracing.

"Wadus, I didn't think it was you. You look like some character out of Tombstone. Wadus, I hope you realize what your call means. I am not going back."

"I had no intention of allowing you to. Now get up." They stood as he reached into the pocket of the long coat and withdrew a small box saying, "I do not have any intention of living with Trina Clark." Taking a small diamond from the box he said, "See if this fits."

She took the ring and silently walked backward just gazing at it. He watched as she began to cry, and he thought of how her beauty seemed to blend perfectly with that of the beach, the song of the surf, and the blueness of the Carolina sky. He took her into his arms and wrapped the long coat around her as he said, "I swear, woman, you are the most crying female I've ever known."

"Oh hush. Wadus, you don't know how many thousands of times I've prayed for this. Just hold me, Wadus. Just hold me, cause I've got something else to tell you. I'm pregnant, or at least I'm 99% sure I am."

"Yes, I know. I found out early this morning."

Trina's head snapped up immediately and she said, "That's impossible, no one knew. How did you find out?"

"The Man above sent his messengers." He laughed as she looked at him as if he were teasing her. He said, "Baby, we'll talk of many things in the future, and as I once told you, you will come to understand it all."

They walked back toward the pier as Trina continued to talk so fast, about so many things, he could only smile and enjoyed the enthusiasm and love he saw. As they reached the gazebo she said, "Wadus, I don't want to work for several years after our baby comes, and I've got it all figured out. I have saved over $200,000, and I have quite a lot of stock, and we can live on this for at least three or four years. Then I'll get a job because I don't want you to ever work again. You've been through too much."

"You've got that much? Huh, that's good. When you soon become Mrs. Wadus Strickland we'll add it to what I have and by my calculations we'll be a little better than millionaires."

Trina stopped talking and looked afraid as she asked, "Are you serious Wadus? Where did you get that much money?"

Wadus laughed loudly and said, "Don't worry, Baby, it's all legal and honest. Or at least as much as that bunch on Wall Street are legal and honest." He placed his hand gently on her stomach and continued, "Now you listen to me young lady, this is the only thing you will ever have to work on again. That is unless more come along cause I don't intend to practice any birth control. We're going to work at loving, raising this child, living and just being unbelievably happy and satisfied."

Trina Clark married Wadus Strickland in a very simple ceremony early in December. This union took place in the gazebo on the strand at Sunset Beach.

Wadus had relied upon the God he believed in and had prayed for a miracle. He now knew God had heard his plea and had responded graciously. Somehow it did not seem he had lost seven years but had gained as many. His Jamie was with God, his true Father, and Wadus now accepted His judgement. He would indeed find his Jamie again when God beckoned. God had worked His will and had bestowed great gifts upon Wadus upon releasing him.

Wadus purchased a small piece of land, cleared it, and installed a new mobile home. He sent the deed, and pictures, with a letter to Mohamet Kabul in Central Prison. The note was short, but the lion of Central Prison turned his huge head to the gray wall and wept when he read, "Dear Friend, this is yours. It is awaiting your arrival. I once told you to have faith. Continue to do so. I will greet you when you walk out of Central."

Mohamet Kabul was paroled in May of 1996 and was embraced by Wadus as he walked through the gates a free man. As they drove away Wadus said, "Mohamet, I want to make one quick stop and say hello to a few people and then we'll go home."

Mohamet was shocked as Wadus stopped at the gates of the Governor's mansion and was allowed to proceed. He drove around to the back and said, "Come on Mohamet, I want to introduce you to a few people you've heard so much about."

Mohamet reluctanly agreed, and as they entered the kitchen the reaction to Mohamet's statue was the same as Wadus's had been the first time he had seen him. Wadus first introduced him to Mrs. Clara who looked up into the face of this giant and exclaimed, "Lawd have mercy. I never seed a youngun lik yo is. Lawd, Lawd, yo makes Snowball look lik ah miget." Mohamet laughed as they spoke briefly, and she made him take one of her fresh buttermilk biscuits.

Shawna had been unusually quiet, and sudued, as she could not take her eyes off of what she saw but could not believe. Wadus said, "Shawna, this is Mohamet Kabul, a very dear friend of mine. Mohamet this is Shawna. She isn't usually this quiet, and she made my years here much brighter."

Shawna extended her hand and Mohamet took it into his as if an adult were holding the hand of a newborn child. She said, "It's a pleasure to meet you. I've heard so much about you from Wadus."

"Thank you ma'am, I've heard a lot about you too. You are even prettier than Wadus said."

Wadus hugged Mrs. Clara, Shawna, said good bye to the others and then said, "Well, Mohamet, we had better be on our way. Shawna, I'll expect you down real soon now so we can all go dancing. When are you coming down? We have lots of room."

Shawna glanced at Mohamet and replied, "Real soon Wadus, real soon."

Shawna did come real soon, and often, as she and Mohamet became very serious about each other. They were married one year later. The lion had conquered himself, gained freedom, had won a precious prize, and was now mighty.

Trina Strickland gave birth to a healthy, beautiful, girl baby on July 6th, 1996. She was named Clara Athena Strickland. She would be schooled to exemplify the kindness, love, and wisdom her name represented.

Mohamet, Shawna, Wadus, Trina, and Clara Athena were blessed and their happiness grew. From time to time the Governor of North Carolina visited his prisoner in his small kingdom by the sea. Neither realized how forged their future destinies were nor that God had not yet released either of them.

IN HOC SIGNO VINCES

THE END

Order Form

To order additional copies, fill out this form and send it along with your check or money order to: Roy Young, 9244 Shady Forest, S.W., Calabash, NC 28467.

Cost per copy $12.95 plus $1.95 P&H. If shipped to an address in North Carolina, include 6% state sales tax.
E-mail: shades@xaranda.net

Ship _____ copies of *The Governor's Prisoner* to:

Name_____

Address:_____

Address:_____

Address:_____

❑ **Check box for signed copy**